ONE MORE TIME!

ONE
MORE
TIME!

◆

Charles Ferry

Houghton Mifflin Company
Boston   1985

The author is indebted to Ted Strasser and Jay Roberts, both of radio station WJR, Detroit, who have helped keep alive an important era in American popular music; to Marvin "Doc" Holiday, jazz specialist at the Oakland University School of Music, Rochester, Michigan; and to Andy Stoffa, formerly of radio station WQRS, Detroit, who is one of the country's foremost authorities on the music and orchestras of the big band era.

The Gene Markham Orchestra's theme song, which is quoted throughout this book, is "Moonlight Cocktail," words and music by Lucky Roberts and Kim Gannon. Copyright © 1941, 1942 by Jewel Music Publishing Co., Inc., New York, N.Y. Used by permission. All rights reserved.

Library of Congress Cataloging in Publication Data

Ferry, Charles, 1927–
  One more time.

  Summary: Skeets Sinclair, the young tenor sax in
Gene Markham's Orchestra, finds his life and the future
of the band changing fast as they tour the United States
during World War II.
  [1. World War, 1939–1945—United States—Fiction.
2. Bands (Music)—Fiction. 3. Musicians—Fiction]
I. Title.
PZ7.F42on 1985   [Fic]   84-20507
ISBN 0-395-36692-5

Printed in the United States of America

S 10 9 8 7 6 5 4 3 2 1

✦ To Jane Bingham ✦

Contents

The Gene Markham Orchestra

BRASS SECTION

Gene Markham, *36, Cedar Rapids, Iowa. Trombone (1st chair)*

Bobby Consiglio, *21, Wichita, Kansas. Trombone*

Eddie McCoy, *21, Ord, Nebraska. Trombone*

Raymond Bootz, *24, Mobridge, South Dakota. Trombone*

Frankie Ciano, *19, Duluth, Minnesota. Trumpet (1st chair)*

Herb Peters, *19, Danville, Illinois. Trumpet*

Mike Zollar, *23, Ann Arbor, Michigan. Trumpet*

Henry Staub, *24, Palatka, Florida. Trumpet*

REED SECTION

Don Rowell, *20, Onley, Virginia. Alto Saxophone (1st chair)*

John Verla, *21, Rehoboth Beach, Delaware. Alto Saxophone*

Skeets (Schuyler) Sinclair, *19, Princess Anne, Virginia. Tenor Saxophone (Lead Clarinet)*

The Gene Markham Orchestra

Dave Waite, *24, Winslow, Arizona. Tenor Saxophone*
A.C. Etter, *22, Abilene, Texas. Baritone Saxophone*

RHYTHM SECTION

Harry Swanson, *19, Poughkeepsie, New York. Piano*
Buddy Glumm, *20, Elkhart, Indiana. String Bass*
Augie Renna, *20, Elkhart, Indiana. Drums*
Jesse Greenhausen, *24, Corvallis, Oregon. Guitar*

VOCALISTS

Polly Breen, *18, Des Plaines, Illinois. Soprano*
   THE MELLOW BIRDS
Hubie Saunders, *21, Marietta, Ohio. First Tenor*
Bernie McCarragher, *22, Shaker Heights, Ohio. Second Tenor*
Mike Chapman, *21, Xenia, Ohio. Baritone*
Bob Krause, *22, Oak Harbor, Ohio. Bass*

OTHER PERSONNEL

Gus Oshinsky, *48, Toledo, Ohio. Road Manager*
Ellen Bowe, *29, Upper Darby, Pennsylvania. Office Manager*
Basil Brandt, *16, Waukesha, Wisconsin. Band Boy*

ONE
MORE
TIME!

·1·
Finality

My second year with the band — the year I stopped being embarrassed about my age — we crisscrossed the country in an endless succession of one-nighters. Misty-eyed couples danced and dreamed to our music, trying to shut out the grim headlines that filled the newspapers.

Coupl'a jiggers of moonlight and add a star,
Pour in the blue of a June night and one guitar.

Time began running out for us one blustery December night in the Galesburg depot. We had played a date at the local college — Knox College — and gotten stranded afterward in a blizzard that howled in off the Illinois prairie — twenty-two musicians and singers, plus Gus Oshinsky, the road manager, and Basil Brandt, our band boy. Snow had drifted up to the windowsills, and the trains to Chicago were running several hours late. And as we huddled around a coal stove in the drafty waiting room, Gene confirmed what our office manager, Ellen Bowe, had hinted before we left New York. He had applied for a commission in the army.

"Lamentoso," I heard Augie Renna mutter. Augie, our drummer, evaluated most situations in musical terms. "Molto lamentoso."

It summed up our reaction. We stared blankly at Gene, waiting for him to go on. He was a tall, lanky man, more like a schoolteacher than a bandleader. He lowered his eyes as if sensing our unasked question. In just two years, we'd gone from fifth place to second in the *Down Beat* poll. We were packing them in from coast to coast. Why quit now, just when we had a chance of making it to the top?

"I really don't have an explanation." He said it quietly, apologetically. "It was just something I felt I had to do."

Harry Swanson and I took the news in stride; we'd been friends and roommates since Juilliard and had weathered a few ups and downs. But Polly Breen, our vocalist, was crushed. The band was the only home she'd ever known.

"Do you think the army will accept him, Skeets?" she asked me.

"I doubt it, Polly," I replied. "He's over thirty-five, and we're not even at war yet."

But I didn't really believe that. I had a premonition that the war was finally catching up to us. And two days later — it did. As we swung south for a week at the Blue Room in New Orleans, newsboys came through the train hawking extras about the Japanese attack on Pearl Harbor.

"Pearl Harbor?" Basil said, puzzled. "Where the heck's that?"

"Beats me," Augie said. He called across the aisle to where Harry and I were playing gin rummy. "Do you guys know?"

"Hawaii," I answered. "It's a big navy base."

Buddy Glumm, our string bass player and Augie's best friend, read the headlines in amazement.

"Why, those dirty astards-bay!" he said. (Buddy was fond of pig latin.) "They sank a bunch of our battleships. I guess we're at war."

"We were bound to get into it, sooner or later," Augie said.

"Well, it won't be much of a war," Harry said. "The only thing the Japs are good at is making cheap toys." He spread his cards out on the suitcase we were using as a table. "Gin, Skeets."

"Yeah, but what if we have to fight the Germans, too?" Basil said.

No one had an answer. Being at war was new to us, and we couldn't quite grasp it. Least of all Polly. It had been just a year ago, at the Palmer House in Chicago, that Sister Angela had brought her in from St. Mary's for an audition. Everybody's kid sister — blonde, leggy, effervescent, with fawnlike eyes and a trace of schoolgirl awkwardness. She'd been on the program at the Coliseum the night before, singing "Moon Love" in a sweet clear voice. Gene had sensed a special magic in her.

"Maybe a little padding in the bra," Gus had suggested.

But Gene wouldn't hear of it. Let Tommy Dorsey and Harry James have the oomph girls, he said; we

3

would have the Girl Next Door. Polly had been just seventeen then; Gene had had to sign as her legal guardian before the court would allow her to leave the orphanage and take the job. She was no match for stars like Peggy Lee or Helen O'Connell, but she had a breathless way of phrasing and a smile that would break your heart. In dozens of star-ceilinged ballrooms, lovesick boys had gazed longingly at her as she threw kisses to the crowd.

> *Mix in a coupl'a dreamers and there you are,*
> *Lovers hail the Moonlight Cocktail.*

It was great box office, but deep down, Polly wasn't show biz. She wanted success, yes; but she wanted roots even more. To her, the band was a family to be looked after. She frequently pressed the trousers of Basil's only suit with the little iron she carried with her on the road — the pants spread out on the tile floor of some hotel bathroom. And whenever Harry or I incurred Gus's wrath, she called us "poor wounded birds" and tried to comfort us.

But after Galesburg, the situation was reversed. It was Polly who needed support. Harry and I made special efforts to cheer her up — as did Gus. A short, dumpy man, whose double-breasted suits always looked baggy, he hovered over her like an anxious father, which helped compensate for Gene's inattention. Gene always seemed to be busy with new arrangements, or on the phone checking bookings with Ellen Bowe, who ran our office back in New York.

"You'd think Old Stone Face would show a little

4

interest in her," Harry griped during a break at the Blue Room. "After all, Gene's her guardian, not Gus."

Gus blew up. "You never learn, do you, wise guy?" he growled. "One more crack like that, and you'll be back at Juilliard practicing scales." He glanced down at Harry's tasseled loafers. "And get those fruity shoes shined before I slap a fine on you."

On our last night in New Orleans, Harry and I treated Polly to a late supper at Brennan's. Polly insisted that we invite Gus — over Harry's protests.

"For Pete's sake, Harry," she said. "Gus isn't the ogre you make him out to be. Why don't you try being nice to him for a change? After all, it isn't easy for him, being away from his wife for months on end."

But Gus couldn't make it. He was expecting a phone call from his son, who was a B-25 pilot stationed at an army air corps base in Florida; and so Basil came with us instead. Basil, who seldom got to eat at a fancy restaurant, had trouble with the menu.

"What's *soupe aux pois*?" he asked.

"Pea soup," I said.

"Heck, we have that all the time at home," he said. "I think I'll have steak with mushrooms."

"Basil, you don't order steak at Brennan's," Harry instructed him. "You order seafood."

We had oysters and pompano and rich black coffee with chicory in it. Polly had never eaten pompano before, or even heard of chicory.

"That's one nice thing about growing up in a place like Saint Mary's. There are so many lovely things to catch up on. I think I'll have cherries jubilee for dessert."

Afterward, we walked in the narrow streets of the

French Quarter, past houses with courtyards and grilled balconies. The night air seemed warm and balmy after the blizzards of Illinois. Inevitably, the conversation got around to the band's future. Basil was even more worried than Polly.

"I don't suppose there's an employment agency for band boys," he said. "Twenty-five bucks ain't much, but my old man was only making thirty a week at the foundry when he died."

"Something'll turn up, Basil," I said. "Talk to Gus."

Harry, whose nonchalance matched his casual good looks, thought we were getting all worked up over nothing. "I'll bet Gene couldn't even pass an army physical," he said.

"He's healthy as a horse, Harry," Polly said. "And you know it."

"Well, so what if we break up?" he said. "After playing with the number two band, it ought to be easy to land good jobs."

"It'd be easier if we were number one," I said.

"When does the new *Down Beat* poll come out?" he asked me.

"Probably not till after we break up," I said. "It won't do us much good then."

"But we'll still be number two, won't we?" he said. "I'll bet the offers'll be pouring in."

"Maybe for you," Polly said. "You're a regular Paderewski on the piano, and Skeets can play any woodwind that was ever invented. It's different with me."

"Aw, come on, Polly," I said. "You were fifth in the last poll, weren't you?"

6

"It's only because of the band, Skeets," she said. "I have no illusions about myself. I'm just a crowd pleaser with a pleasant voice. Besides, I'm not sure what I want to do. I've watched the older girls in the business. It's made them hard."

"Well, for crying out loud, Pols," Harry said. "What do you want to do — live on a farm and wear gingham dresses?"

"Oh, I don't know," she said, and steered us away from Rampart Street. "Come on, let's get back before you and Skeets decide to close up the jazz joints."

"But I've never been to a jazz joint," Basil said.

"And you're not going to," Polly said. "Until you're eighteen."

On the trip back to New York, a fine holiday spirit filled the train. Gene threw an eggnog party in the diner, at which Gus passed out our Christmas checks. And that night, Polly and the Mellow Birds, the four crew-cut boys from Ohio State who made up the band's vocal group, sang carols in the club car. We had drinks and talked of our holiday plans. (Club car waiters seldom checked your age; normally those of us under twenty-one had to rely on phony IDs.) We would be getting a Christmas break before settling down for the winter at the Emerald Room of the Hotel Vanderbilt, which was our home, to the extent that a traveling dance orchestra could have a home. We would go back out on the road in the spring — if the band still existed then.

"Don't worry, we're not going to break up," Harry kept assuring everyone. "Mark my words."

And so when we arrived in New York, there were happy good-byes at Grand Central Station. I was going

home to Virginia, to the little town of Princess Anne —
reluctantly, for my father had never accepted my career
in music. Ellen had invited Gene to her parents' home
in Upper Darby, near Philadelphia. Harry would be
going up to Poughkeepsie; his girl, Sarah, would be
home from college, and there would be a big family
dinner and many parties.

"But I thought you and Sarah had broken up," Polly
said.

"Think again," Harry said. "Sarah keeps hounding
me to go to law school, but otherwise she's a good kid."

Augie and Buddy canceled a trip home to Elkhart,
Indiana, when a Christmas invitation arrived from the
Beasley sisters, identical twins they'd met when we
played a one-nighter in Brooklyn. Buddy, a short,
squarely built boy, was elated.

"This could mean spring time," he said to Augie,
elbowing him and grinning lewdly. (To Augie and
Buddy, "spring time" alluded to bedsprings, not the
season, and meant any girl who offered erotic possibilities.) But Augie, who was teaching Basil how to
play the drums, had other ideas.

"With their parents in the house?" he said. "Forget
it. Let's ask them if we can bring Basil."

"Are you kidding?" Buddy said. "Just when we
finally get a chance to go the distance with Dora and
Donna?"

"But the kid can't afford a trip home to Wisconsin,"
Augie persisted. "And a hotel's a lousy place to spend
Christmas."

"Well — okay," Buddy agreed, but added an important stipulation. "If we tell you to scram," he told Basil, "am-scray."

"Gee, thanks, guys," Basil said with a wide smile. "I won't cramp your style, Buddy. I know how it is in springtime."

Buddy broke into laughter. "Listen to the squirt," he said. "Not seventeen yet, and he's telling me the score."

Polly was spending the holidays in Toledo with Gus and his family — his wife, Sadie, and his son, Bert. Harry razzed Polly about Bert the day we saw her off.

"Better watch out for that fly-boy, Pols. You might end up one of the family."

"And what would be wrong with that?" She smiled pertly. "He might be a dreamboat and sweep me off my feet."

"Oh, yeah?" Harry grinned. "And what if he looks like Gus?"

"Harry!" She glanced around, but Gus had gone on ahead with the luggage. "Honestly, one of these days Gus is going to brain you."

"Who cares?" Harry shrugged. "He's already fined me into bankruptcy."

We said good-bye, and Polly started through the gate. She was wearing a belted blue coat with matching knee socks, and looked more like a freshman at Vassar than a vocalist with a dance band. She waved as she hurried down the ramp. Then suddenly she ran back and took my hand.

"You've been wonderful, Skeets," she said, out of breath. "I hope everything's all right at home."

My heart did flip-flops. Half the band was in love with Polly, of course. But I was in love with her *seriously* — and hopelessly, for I was short, unexciting, and wore horn-rimmed glasses with thick lenses. But there was an important consolation. My lack of prospects gave me her friendship in a special way, and I treasured it.

"Have a good trip, Polly," I said. "And no worrying. Promise?"

"Yes, Skeets. I promise."

"Merry Christmas, Polly."

"Merry Christmas, Skeets."

And that's the way it was, sixteen days after Pearl Harbor. The newspapers were filled with grim headlines, as they would be for months to come. We were now at war with both Japan and Germany. The Japanese had seized control of half the Pacific. The U.S. outposts of Guam and Wake Island had fallen. In the Philippines, remnants of our army were retreating into the Bataan Peninsula.

But we didn't pay much attention to the war. Our engagement at the Vanderbilt flew by with no word about Gene's commission, and we began to think we'd been reprieved. Then on our last night, with the waiters stacking the chairs and all of us gathered around, Gene told us what nobody wanted to hear.

"I've heard from the army," he said. "I'm to report in June, a week after we get back from the tour —"

He paused, as if not knowing what to say next. A vacuum cleaner hummed from the lobby. "That won't leave you much time to line up jobs," he went on. "So I'll leave it up to you. Anyone who thinks we ought to cancel the tour, raise your hand."

No hands were raised. Gene smiled, a bit proudly, I thought.

"What's our itinerary?" asked Frankie Ciano, who played lead trumpet.

"The usual," Gene said. "New England first, and then we'll work our way west to California."

"Are we booked for the Panther Room?" asked John Verla, alto saxophone. "I left some shirts at a laundry in Chicago."

"We'll have two nights at the Panther Room," Gene replied. "Gus, do you have the dates?"

Gus, chewing on his unlighted cigar, thumbed through the sheets on his clipboard.

"May fourteenth and fifteenth," he said. "We'll have a day off in Chicago and then play a prom at the University of Illinois." He flipped to the next sheet. "Oh, yeah, another thing. We'll be playing a lot of military bases and war bond rallies, some of them pretty early in the morning. I don't want to hear any bitching, understand? Consider it your patriotic bit for the war effort."

"Tell that to my draft board," said Hubie Saunders, who sang first tenor with the Mellow Birds. "Maybe they'll give me a deferment."

"Any other questions?" Gene asked us.

There weren't.

"Okay, I guess that's it," he said. "Tomorrow's a day off. RCA wants us for a recording session the day after. The tour starts as soon as we finish."

And then he and Gus left. The rest of us milled around the floor for a while, trying to absorb what had happened. Basil folded our music stands and started disassembling Augie's trap drums, taking care to loosen the catgut strings on the bottom drumhead of the snare drum. Augie gave him a hand with the big bass drum, pausing to beat out a dirgelike roll on it, with his hands, as they packed it.

"A coda," he said, shaking his head sadly. "The damn tour's going to be one long gloomy coda."

None of us felt like sleeping that night. Augie, Buddy, and A.C. Etter, who played baritone sax, decided to go down to a jazz place in Greenwich Village.

"A real hot combo's playing there," A.C. said. "The guy on vibes is as good as Lionel Hampton."

Polly and Harry and I strolled over to an all-night coffee place opposite Penn Station. It was three A.M. The streets had been freshly sprayed, and the produce trucks were making their rounds. Polly reminisced about the time I squeaked a high note on one of our radio shows, and the time Harry and I stuffed toilet paper into the bell of Gene's trombone.

"The crazy things you do," Harry said.

"Maybe he'll form another band after the war," Polly said.

"Maybe," I said. "But it wouldn't be the same."

The horn of a freighter, deep and resonant, sounded from over on the Hudson River.

"No," she said quietly. "I suppose it wouldn't."

·2·
A Combo?

A fan magazine had once run an article on Polly and her "glamorous" life with the Gene Markham Orchestra. The spread had included a photograph of her, in her white chiffon gown, singing "Stardust" at a county fair in Iowa. Polly thought it was hilarious.

"Glamorous?" she said. "We had to dress in the bus that night and sleep in it afterward, and I got manure all over my shoes during intermission."

Living conditions on a road tour involved extremes — one day an elegant hotel, the next day no clean sheets, no warm bath, and a greasy meal at some all-night diner. But the road offered one important advantage: Our meals and lodgings were paid for by Gene as a business expense. During our long engagements at the Vanderbilt, however, we were on our own. Some of the married sidemen — eight of our musicians had brought their wives to New York — rented furnished rooms near the hotel. Eddie McCoy, third trombone, whose young wife was expecting their first baby, had a little apartment in Jackson Heights, where a few of us got together occasionally for jam sessions. For the rest of us, Gene had struck a deal with the hotel management. We could rent rooms in a special fourteenth-floor wing and eat in the coffee shop, both at substantial discounts. Basil had the best deal of all, free meals in the coffee shop and a fold-up bed in Gus's room, also free.

"It's a pretty classy setup," Basil said. "Gus even tutors me in math."

Basil, a bouncy, cheerful boy, was from Waukesha, a small town in the dairy country of Wisconsin. He had come into our lives ten months ago, in the spring of 1941, when we were playing the Schroeder Hotel in Milwaukee. He had skipped school and hitchhiked to Milwaukee, looking for a job as band boy. Our current band boy had just been hired away by Guy Lombardo's orchestra and would be leaving in two weeks. Gus was impressed by Basil's eager manner but doubtful about his age.

"Tell me the truth, kid," he said in his gruff way, "are you really seventeen?"

Basil's face turned a little red. "Well, almost," he said. "I've got a birthday coming up in a few weeks."

"I think I'd better phone your mother," Gus said.

"We don't have a phone," Basil said quickly. "We're sort of poor."

But he had mentioned that his mother worked part-time at a laundry. Gus called information for the number of every laundry in Waukesha — there were only four — and soon had Mrs. Brandt on the phone.

"You're a lousy liar, kid," he reported. "You've got a birthday coming up, all right, but it's your sixteenth, not your seventeenth. Your mother thought you were in school, where you belong."

But Basil got the job. Gus had learned that Basil's father, who had been in and out of work throughout the Depression, had died just a month after he landed a steady job. Mrs. Brandt was struggling to keep the family going — Basil and his two younger sisters — working at the laundry and taking in sewing.

"But there's one condition," Gus told Basil sternly. "You've got to keep up your studies. Your mother's sending your school books and some clean underwear over on the interurban train."

"Gee, thanks, Mr. Oshinsky," Basil said, beaming. "You won't regret it. I'm a fast learner."

"So I've noticed," Gus said dryly.

Basil turned out to be the best band boy we'd ever had, getting us set up quickly for dates, always placing the microphones correctly, devising a better way to pack our books. Soon Gus was relying on him to check the gate (promoters sometimes tried to cheat us), stationing him near the box office with a counter, so that Basil could click off the patrons as they bought tickets.

"The kid's clever," Gus said. "He blends into the crowd, and no one's the wiser."

Basil was a clearinghouse for band gossip, and after Pearl Harbor he became our chief source of war news. The night Polly and Harry and I had coffee at the place near Penn Station, Basil was still up when we got back to the hotel — curled up in a big armchair in the lobby, reading the newspaper.

"Honestly, Basil," Polly said. "Don't you ever sleep?"

Basil yawned. "Somebody's got to keep up with the war," he said.

"How's the war going?" Harry asked him.

"Lousy," Basil said. "Things aren't so good on the home front, either. They're going to start rationing a bunch more things."

"What now?" I said. "They're already rationing gasoline and tires."

"Meat, coffee, butter, cheese," Basil said. "Even silk stockings."

"Swell," Polly said. "And I'm down to my last pair."

It was nearly five o'clock when we went up to our rooms; in a dance band, you got used to going to bed at dawn. As we walked to the elevator, we passed several soldiers, who, unable to find hotel rooms, had slept in the lobby, sprawled out on couches. A few of them cast hostile glances at Harry and me.

"I wish they wouldn't stare at us like that," I said. We were still wearing our band uniforms, dark blue jackets and pale blue trousers, with polka-dot bow ties. "I feel like some kind of freak."

"Relax, Skeeter," Harry said nonchalantly. "They'd love to trade places with us."

Harry and I still hadn't given much thought to the war. For the time being, I was classified 4-F in the draft, because of my eyes. Augie and Buddy were both I-A, which meant they might be called up at any time. Harry should have been I-A, but had been deferred. A man on the Poughkeepsie draft board was trying to curry favor with Harry's father, who was an influential attorney. Henry Staub, who played fourth trumpet, had dubbed Harry "our resident draft dodger." But I had a feeling that we were both on borrowed time.

"I don't know, Harry," I said as we got off at the fourteenth floor. "Sometimes I think we're out of step."

"How do you figure that, for Pete's sake?" Harry asked. "*Every*body can't be in the service."

"No," I agreed, "but a dance band isn't exactly a critical industry."

"I wouldn't say that, Skeeter," Harry said. "We've got to keep up morale on the home front."

Our room had a fine view of the sun rising over Long Island. I was hoping that Harry might want to stay up and talk, but he got right into his pajamas and crawled into bed. "Close the blinds, will you, Skeeter?" he said. "I don't want the bright sun to ruin my beauty sleep."

Harry, I had learned, could sleep through any crisis. I closed the blinds, stripped down to my shorts, and reached under my bed for the Manila folder with my lined music paper and the special fountain pen that I used for writing music. I was making my first efforts at composing — a piano concerto in ragtime and a symphonic suite that had a good opening but was lacking a suitable theme for the *largo*.

But the events of the day had left me in a gloomy frame of mind, and my brain just wouldn't work. And so with Harry snoring contentedly, I sat crosslegged on the floor, fiddling with my fountain pen, a souvenir of the 1939 New York World's Fair, which Harry and I had visited when we were still at Juilliard.

Harry and I had been what is known as prodigies, although we both hated the term. Harry was playing Chopin sonatas when he was six; I had first displayed my talent for music in kindergarten. We had each skipped two grades in elementary school, were fifteen when we graduated from prep school and seventeen when we finished at Juilliard, where we developed a growing interest in jazz and swing.

We had been great fans of the Gene Markham Orchestra. Harry had all of the band's records; we had played them so often, we'd memorized the arrangements. Shortly before graduation, we borrowed a classmate's old Model A Ford and drove over to Cedar Grove, New Jersey, to Frank Dailey's Meadowbrook, a big, rustic night spot where the band was playing. We posed as autograph seekers, and then hit Gene up for a job. He was polite, but abrupt.

"What instruments do you play?" he asked us.

"Piano," Harry said.

"Any woodwind," I said.

"That covers a lot of territory," he said. "Saxophone? Clarinet?"

"Both," I said. "Clarinet is my favorite, but I play a pretty good tenor sax."

"Well, I can't talk to you now," he said. "Come backstage during intermission."

We talked to Gene backstage for a few minutes, but nothing came of it. He told us to leave our names and addresses with Gus, and that was that.

"I don't think we made a very good impression on him," I said.

"Nothing ventured," Harry said, shrugging, "nothing gained."

We returned to school with little to show for the experience, except two autographs, on the backs of our

Juilliard ID cards, which we flashed around campus. Harry thought we ought to try for jobs with a pit orchestra on Broadway, or maybe a studio orchestra at one of the radio networks.

"If we could just get an audition, I'll bet we'd get hired," he said. "That's what queered it with Gene — no audition."

I gave my graduation recital on a Sunday afternoon, in Juilliard's main recital hall, before a small audience. I had chosen the clarinet solo from Respighi's *Pines of Rome*, with Harry accompanying me on the piano. I was in a long crescendo when I saw Gene Markham and Gus Oshinsky slip into the hall and take seats in the back row. I nearly gulped. Harry had also seen them come in. *"Let's give 'em an audition,"* he whispered to me, and began adding little flourishes of jazz to his accompaniment. We ended up playing Respighi in four-four time.

"Very good, Schuyler," Gene said to me afterward. "A little sloppy on the crescendo, but you pulled it together."

"I got nervous when I saw you come in," I said.

"I thought I'd audition the two of you on your own home ground," he said, and turned to Harry. "You did those chromatic *glissandos* very well."

Gene wasted no time in getting down to business. "We're anticipating some openings," he said. "Are you both free to travel?"

"Are we ever!" I said excitedly.

He wanted me for third saxophone and lead clarinet, he said. I knew that everyone in his five-man reed section doubled on clarinet, but he thought my tone was right for a new sound he was working on.

"Do you own a tenor sax?" he asked me.

"No, sir," I replied. "Just a clarinet."

"See the Carstairs Company over on West Forty-fifth Street," he said. "They'll fix you up at a good price. Now if you'll excuse me, there's a friend on the faculty I want to look up. Gus will handle the details."

From the beginning, Harry didn't hit it off with Gus. "Fifty-five bucks a week to start," Gus said. "Five bucks extra when we're on the road."

"Fifty-five?" Harry said. "Benny Goodman starts his sidemen at sixty-five."

"Then call up Benny and get yourself a job, wise guy," Gus growled. He handed each of us a little mimeographed booklet. "Here are the rules and regulations. Cross me up, and you're in bad trouble."

"When do we start?" I asked him.

"We'll give you a call," he said. "I'll have our band boy drop off copies of the piano and third sax books. Memorize them."

We did. We also memorized the rule book. At least I did; Harry thought it was petty and unrealistic.

"I'd heard that Gene runs a chicken outfit," he said, "but this is ridiculous. You practically have to raise your hand to go to the bathroom."

We were expected to show up for a date on time, in clean white shirts, with our shoes shined, our uniforms pressed, and our neckties knotted properly. We were to be clean shaven, have a proper haircut (long hair was forbidden, as were gaudy socks), and keep both feet on the floor when playing. Fines ranged from fifty cents to five dollars. The stiffest fines involved drinking or being late for rehearsal. When we played nightclubs, we were to stay out of the bar (drinks were seldom served at ballrooms). And if you missed a train or a bus, you were automatically fired.

"I wonder if we're *allowed* to go to the bathroom," Harry said.

I spent an afternoon trying out used tenor saxophones, finally settling on a fine instrument that had belonged to a well-known jazz saxist. Gus called the next day, and within two weeks, Harry and I were on a bus to Atlantic City, where the band was playing a one-week engagement at the Steel Pier. I was very nervous during the first set, but relaxed when I found I could easily handle the arrangements. Harry and I soon learned that Gene demanded precision performance. Although he was a working bandleader — he played first trombone — nothing went by him.

"Observe the markings!" he admonished Harry after he'd come in two beats late on "A String of Pearls," and to me, "You're not getting the phrasing right on 'Deep Purple,' Skeets. More *appassionato*."

I had worried that Harry and I might be looked down on by the other sidemen because of our age. I needn't have. Age meant nothing; talent was everything. Many of the greats in the business had been playing professionally in their early teens. Benny Goodman, "the King of Swing," was playing a hot clarinet when he was in eighth grade; and Fats Waller, the great jazz pianist, was even younger when he entertained in theaters in Harlem.

Still, even in a youthful business, Gene had put together a band of unusually young — and gifted — musicians. Frankie Ciano, who had been sixteen when Gene discovered him playing in a high-school combo in Duluth, Minnesota, could blow a hundred high C's in a row and top them off with an even higher F; and Don Rowell, lead sax, who had joined the band at age seventeen, had a fine harmonic awareness that I knew I could never match.

"That kid who plays second trumpet," Harry said to me at lunch one day. "The one with pimples."

"Herb Peters?" I said.

"Yeah. Well, I saw him walking down the boardwalk this morning, carrying a stuffed animal and sucking on a lollipop. This band's a regular kiddie farm."

There was a reason for Gene's emphasis on youth, we would learn later. His first band had been built around a core of more seasoned musicians, who turned out to be undisciplined boozers. Drinking had killed the band and wiped Gene out financially. He was determined not to make the same mistake twice. And so when he found backing for a second band, he looked for young musicians to mold into the kind of orchestra he wanted. This probably explains his interest in Harry and me: we hadn't had a chance to pick up bad habits.

Only two of the others had conservatory training: Raymond Bootz, fourth trombone, was a graduate of the Eastman School of Music, and Jesse Greenhausen, guitarist, had studied classical guitar at the Oberlin

Conservatory. The rest had attached themselves to experienced musicians in their communities and received an education they never would have gotten in a classroom. Gene had recruited them wherever he found them, in college combos, in high-school marching bands, in small-town jazz joints. He had found Augie and Buddy playing in a Dixieland group at a roadhouse outside of Elkhart — on instruments borrowed from their high school's music department.

"But we don't own our instruments," Augie said.

"We'll buy trap drums and a string bass as a band expense," Gene said. "You'll play them, but the band will own them."

Harry and I quickly became fast friends with Augie and Buddy, whose good spirits always gave us a boost. When Polly joined the band, she gravitated to our circle, as did Basil. Wherever Augie was, Basil was never far away. The day after Gene gave us the bad news about his commission, Basil was tagging along when Augie, Buddy, and Polly came by our room. Harry and I had slept till 4:00 P.M. During our last week at the Vanderbilt, we had also been booked into the Paramount Theater in Times Square. (In most large cities, the big downtown movie houses also ran stage shows, usually a big band.) The pace had been grueling.

"Dave Waite's got a job with Stan Kenton," Augie told us. "He starts when we get back from the tour."

"If he beats the draft, that is," Buddy said.

Augie, a tall, slender boy, went to the dresser mirror and smoothed back his dark hair, which he wore in a pompadour, slicked down with brilliantine.

"You guys done anything about lining up jobs?" he asked Harry and me.

"Not a thing," I said.

"Neither have we," he said. "What about you, Polly?"

"I haven't even thought about it," she replied. "I still can't believe we're breaking up."

"I know what all of you ought to do," Basil said. "Form your own combo."

"Are you kidding?" Buddy said.

"I'm serious," Basil said. "You've got the right combination — piano, bass, and drums, with Skeets soloing on sax or clarinet and Polly on vocals. You'd be a quintet."

"And I suppose we'd need a band boy," Buddy said.

"Wel-l, now that you mention it," Basil said. "You wouldn't want to strain yourself lugging around a big bass fiddle."

"Nice try, Basil," Augie said. "But I couldn't come up with enough dough for a set of drums, let alone the money it'd take for a combo."

"If you and Buddy didn't spend so much money chasing girls," Basil said, "you could afford some drums."

"First things first," Buddy said.

Augie and Buddy were dressed for dates — the Beasley twins again. They'd struck out at Christmas, but hadn't stopped trying.

"We're not picking them up till eight," Augie said. "What say we all have dinner together?"

"Where?" I asked him.

"Pasquale's," he said. "I'm in the mood for spaghetti."

"I'd better get a sweater," Polly said.

"You go with her, Skeeter," Harry said. "We'll meet you in the lobby."

Polly's room was at the far end of our wing. While she combed her hair and put on a blue cardigan, I gazed out the window. It was dusk, but few lights were showing. The tower of the Empire State Building was unlighted, and there was no neon glare in the streets. Since Pearl Harbor, a dimout had been imposed in all coastal cities as a precaution against air raids. Also, the city lights could silhouette our merchant ships and make them easy targets for German submarines.

"It's kind of scary, isn't it?" Polly said, coming to the window and looking over my shoulder. "No glittering skyline."

"Feeling blue?" I asked her.

"I guess so," she said. "This is our last night in the Vanderbilt."

"We'll be here again," I said. "For the farewell performance."

"But everything will be finished then. Here" — she handed me a letter to put in my pocket — "make sure I mail it. It's to Sister Angela. We'll have a day off in Chicago, and I'll be able to get out to Saint Mary's for a visit."

"Things are looking up," I said. "A homecoming."

"Yes," she said, and smiled. "I've missed her so much."

At Pasquale's, where we ran into friends from Sammy

Kaye's orchestra, we ended up having a little party. Harry ordered a bottle of Chianti, and even Polly had a few sips. By the time we started back to the hotel, her spirits had improved.

"At least we've still got the tour," she said as we crossed Fifth Avenue. "You know what Gus says about the road — you never know what's going to happen next."

·3·
Poor Butterfly

The next day we went out on the road for the last time. We had been on a tight schedule all day — morning rehearsal, afternoon recording session (six sides), and then the mad dash to Grand Central to catch the evening express to Albany. It was always a lovely trip, the train curving up the Hudson River, with the blue-tinted highlands of the Catskills rising in the west. Gus, chomping on a cigar, came through our car issuing orders like a carnival barker, which he'd once been.

"Okay, okay, pay attention. There'll be a chartered bus at the depot in Albany. We'll have only an hour to get out to the ballroom and get set up, so hustle your bustles."

"Which outfits?" Buddy asked.

Gus consulted his clipboard.

"Red jackets and gray trousers for the band," he said. "Two-tone blue for the Mellow Birds, and pink satin for Polly."

Ellen Bowe, our office manager, had mimeographed copies of our New England itinerary, which Gus passed around. From Albany, we would backtrack to Connecticut for six shows at the State Theater in Hartford, then a one-nighter in Pittsfield, a spring hop at Amherst College, and two nights at the Starlite Roof in Providence. We wouldn't have a day off until we played the Raymor Ballroom in Boston.

"When do we get to take a bath?" Polly asked.

"Providence," Gus answered. "We've got rooms at the Knickerbocker."

"Providence?" Harry complained. "We'll be scroungy by then. That's the trouble with this lousy outfit. No consideration for the talent, just rake in the cash and the hell with us."

Gus poked his cigar at Harry. "Okay, wise guy," he barked. "You just mouthed yourself into a two-buck fine."

"Two bucks?" Harry protested. "For what?"

"Bad manners, that's what," Gus said. "And if you're so much as two seconds late on the stand tonight, it'll be five bucks."

"Why of all the —" Harry turned to Polly and me. "See how he picks on me?" he said. "Pick, pick, pick."

"Stop your griping, Harry," Polly said. "You're never on time, and you know it."

"Well, so what?" he said. "It's suffocating, the way Gus runs things. Did you read what Weintraub called us in *Metronome*? 'The All-American Boys.' And he's right. Be-on-time-shine-your-shoes-stay-out-of-the-bars. Worst of all, Gene never lets us swing. It cramps your style. Musicians need a little . . . a little —" He snapped his fingers at me. "Skeeter, what am I trying to say?"

"A little creative flexibility," I said.

"Exactly." Harry loosened his tie and slouched into

28

his seat. "Well, eight more weeks and we can tell Gus to take a flying leap."

Polly gave him a cross look. "Harry," she said, "do you have to keep reminding us that we're breaking up?"

"Stop feeling so blue, Pols," he said. "Bands break up all the time, and the sun still rises in the east. I think I'll go home and just lie around for a month. What about you, Skeeter?"

"Not me," I said. "My father would keep bugging me to go in with him at the lumberyard."

"I thought he'd finally gotten off that kick," Harry said.

"He doesn't say much anymore," I said. "But you can feel it."

Basil shook his head. "I don't understand," he said. "If I'd played drums with a big band, my old man would've bragged about it all over Waukesha."

The train raced up the Hudson. It was early evening, and lights were coming on in houses across the river. Gene, who was sitting in the rear of the car, sent word that he wanted to talk to Polly; and Gus asked Basil to go up to the baggage car and make sure our equipment could be quickly unloaded. Augie and Buddy slipped into their seats.

"Remember that crazy idea of Basil's yesterday?" Augie said.

"About forming a combo?" I asked.

"Yeah," he said. "Well, maybe it's not so crazy after all."

"It's a great idea," Harry said. "If we were rolling in dough."

29

"Maybe we could get regular jobs for a while," Buddy said, "and save money that way. Some of the war plants are paying over a buck an hour, with plenty of overtime."

"We'd need an arranger," Augie said.

"I could do the arranging," I said. "I was strong in theory and harmony at Juilliard."

"Could you come up with a cost estimate, Skeets?" Buddy said. "You're good at that sort of stuff, too."

"You guys are whistling Dixie," Harry said. "You don't even own your own instruments."

"But it's worth looking into," Augie said. "What have we got to lose? Okay, Skeets?"

"Okay," I agreed. "When I get the time."

Augie and Buddy wandered off to find a card game. When Polly returned, she seemed more relaxed. Harry pumped her for information.

"Did Gene say anything about paying us a bonus after the tour?" he asked.

"No, but he told me something else." Polly smiled. "Guess what? Ellen's going to join the tour."

"When?" I said.

"As soon as she catches up at the office."

"I'll bet Gus cooked it up," I said. "He's playing Cupid again."

"Well, he's wasting his time," Harry said. "Gene's married to his music. How many times has he left Ellen stranded at the altar? Three?"

"Oh, Harry, it was only twice," Polly said. "And he didn't leave her stranded. There was a mix-up in the bookings."

"Maybe," Harry said. "But he's still a bachelor, isn't he?"

The train was slowing. *"Station stop Al-l-bany!"* the conductor called out. Gus came down the aisle with his clipboard.

"Everybody up and at 'em!"

The ballroom was on the outskirts of the city, an ornate room, with amber lights and a vaulted ceiling. A veranda overlooked the river. Gene was mobbed for autographs as we hurried to the stage entrance. It was a new attendance record, the manager told us, and hundreds had been turned away.

"Can you run some electrical outlets to the veranda?" Gene asked him.

"Of course," he replied. "Why?"

"We'll do two sets out here," Gene said. "I don't want anyone turned away." He turned to Basil. "Move us out here after the second set. We'll all give you a hand."

Basil set a record getting our books and music stands unpacked. There was the usual nervousness and confusion as we hurried to our places. Then at precisely nine o'clock, an off-stage announcer waved Gene a cue. The house lights dimmed, a blue spotlight shone on Gene, and we went into our theme.

"Ladies and gentlemen — the Gene Markham Orchestra, featuring Polly Breen and the Mellow Birds."

The music flooded out in vivid harmonic colors. Saxophones wailed, trombones throbbed, and pretty girls in organdy dresses glided mistily into the arms of their dates.

31

Now add a coupl'a flowers, a drop of dew,
Stir for a coupl'a hours till dreams come true,
As to the number of kisses, it's up to you,
Moonlight cocktails need a few.

It was a large orchestra, capable of remarkable richness and precision — five reeds, four trumpets, four trombones, piano, bass, drums, guitar. Our rhythm section was considered the best in the business, but it was the reeds that gave us our distinctive sound. Arrangements were scored for four saxophones and one clarinet, in a sweeping *legato* style, with the muted brass shimmering in the background and my clarinet carrying the melody high and clear above the saxes. It was a sound other bands could never duplicate, because it wasn't just the reeds. It was the brilliance of the trumpets and the deep, boowahhing undertones of the trombones. It was Polly's charm and freshness, backed by the dreamy motifs of the Mellow Birds. We had our special trademarks. "Medley Time" was one of them; and that night, as Gene stepped to the microphone, the crowd stopped dancing and gathered round the bandstand.

"Something old and new, borrowed and blue. And here with a fine old tune about a 'Poor Butterfly' is our own lovely butterfly, Polly Breen."

Polly had a way of tapping her foot when she sang. That night she didn't, and I thought she looked a trifle wan. But after the last set, she seemed full of energy, and I put it out of my mind.

"Was I imagining it," Harry said as we hurried to

the bus, "or was Old Stone Face a little nostalgic
tonight?"

"You noticed it, too?" Augie said. "He probably feels
sad that it's our last tour."

"It doesn't figure," Harry said. "You can't squeeze
sentiment out of granite."

We piled aboard the bus. It was an old Trailways,
with deep leather seats and curtained windows. As
usual, Polly and I took seats above one of the rear
wheel wells, which allowed more leg room. Augie and
Buddy preferred front seats, as did Basil. Harry made
a beeline for his regular spot, the wide seat at the very
rear.

"Snag me a pillow, Pols," he called to Polly.

"Snag it yourself, Harry," she retorted. "Of all the
nerve. Does Sarah snag pillows for you?"

"Sarah and I haven't progressed to pillows yet," he
said, and winked. "But it won't be long. I'm going to
pop the question."

"That'll be the day," Polly scoffed.

"Oh, yeah?" Harry took a little jeweler's box from
his breast pocket and handed it to her. "Take a
look."

"I don't believe it!" Polly exclaimed.

"Pretty snazzy, Harry," Basil said.

"Snazzy?" Buddy said. "It's stunning. Take a look,
Augie."

Augie held the ring up to the light, squinting at it
with one eye, like a jeweler. "Bellissimo," he said.

"It looks expensive, Harry," I said. "Is it paid for?"

"Are you kidding? The way Gus slaps those fines

around, I was lucky to come up with the down payment."

"Does Sarah know you've bought it?" Polly asked him.

"She will when we get to Boston," Harry said. "She's coming in from Beverly on our night off. I'm fixing Skeeter up with her roommate."

Polly gave him a puzzled look. "Sometimes I just don't understand you, Harry," she said. "You and Sarah have been fighting like cats, and now you're in hock for a diamond."

"I don't know," Harry said with a shrug. "With the war and all, I figure a guy ought to grab hold of something solid."

He yawned and stretched out in the seat.

"Wake me if Benny Goodman calls," he said — and was asleep.

The bus was moving out of the parking lot. When we had all settled down, the driver turned out the interior lights, except for a little night light up front. Polly rested her head on my shoulder.

"Wouldn't you rather sit by the window?" I asked her.

"No, thank you, Skeets. It's a little drafty, and Gus will kill me if I come down with laryngitis again."

The lights of the city fell away. Slowly, the inevitable loneliness of the road set in. It was as though the excitement of the past twenty-four hours had been an illusion, and now the only reality was the bus and the night and the uncertainty of the future. My jacket, which was a size too large, kept bunching up under my arms.

"Take it off," Polly suggested. "I'll put it up in the luggage rack."

She stood on her toes to reach the rack, and as she did so, her knees began to tremble and her breath came quickly. Her face was pale and drawn in the gray light, and there was a twitching in her cheek. And then she was falling, keeling forward across my lap.

"Polly," I whispered. "What's wrong?"

I pulled her into a sitting position and patted her cheeks.

"Polly!"

Slowly, her eyes came open. "What happened?" she said in a weak voice.

"You fainted, I guess. Are you ill?"

"I don't know . . . I felt dizzy and then —" She felt the back of her dress and began to cry. "Oh, Skeets, it's all wet. I feel so embarrassed."

"It's all right, Polly. You lose control when you faint."

"But everyone will know."

"No, they're all asleep. I'll ask the driver to stop at the first gas station that's open. But I'd better tell Gus. You can see a doctor before the first show in Hartford."

"No, don't," she said. "I'm just tired, Skeets. It's been such a frantic day."

"Polly, is there something you're holding back?"

"No . . . Yes . . ." She gave a deep sigh. "I'm so exhausted. I'll tell you about it in Boston, on our night off. All right?"

I agreed, reluctantly, hoping to have a long talk with her before then. As the tour continued, I watched her closely for signs of fatigue. In Pittsfield, my heart

leaped when she stumbled coming onstage; but a tangle
of electrical wires had been left on the floor, and she
quickly regained her balance.

"Relax, Skeets," she said afterward. "I'm just fine.
Really."

She seemed full of energy and performed marvel-
ously, even though the schedule was hectic. We had
hoped this last tour would be a breeze; Gene, however,
had other ideas. The drive for perfection never let up.
Rehearse, rehearse, rehearse. New arrangements to be
learned, war bond rallies and military bases to be
squeezed in. And every Monday, Wednesday, and Friday, the producer of our network show would material-
ize with a script and a stopwatch, which meant even
more rehearsal. All of our broadcasts were live, and if
the early broadcast didn't come off flawlessly, there
would be still more rehearsal before the repeat broadcast for the West Coast three hours later.

"There's gotta be an easier way," Buddy said wearily
one night.

"There is," Augie said. "Our own combo."

"Let's have a standing rule," Buddy said. "Only one
performance a day. The army oughta give us a medal
for all the free entertainment we're giving the troops."

The military shows turned out to be the most enjoy-
able of the tour. The homesick GIs and sailors were
always overjoyed to see us. Polly, predictably, was their
big favorite. At an army camp near Chicopee, she received a hand-carved plaque, certifying that the regi-
ment had voted her the girl they'd most like to share a
foxhole with. At the submarine base in New London,

the atmosphere was so friendly, I thought that Gene wouldn't mind if I improvised a solo on "Tuxedo Junction." I was wrong.

"Observe the markings!" he fumed afterward. "They are there for a purpose."

"But I was only trying to put a little swing into it, Gene," I said. "After all, we get tired of reading stuff like this."

I pulled out a column by Weintraub, the *Metronome* critic, which had concluded with a devastating barb: *"On balance, a great band. Pity they can't swing."*

The column hurt, because it was partly true. We were what was known as a "sweet" band. We knew we could swing with the best of them, but Gene always kept the brakes on. We could go only to the brink of soaring, improvised swing that let every sideman give his best. As a result, we fell short of the smooth, gliding beat of Benny Goodman or the rich, brassy style of Count Basie. Gene gave me a cold look.

"The fans don't seem to mind, do they, Skeets?"

"No, but —"

"And your hero Koussevitzky — does he let his men improvise?"

"Well, no, but —"

"Observe the markings!"

It was difficult to argue with the commercial wisdom of Gene's approach. The headlines in *Variety* told the story:

MARKHAM BAND DOING
BOFFO BIZ ON ROAD!

The crowds had never been bigger, and the band had never played better, which gave Gene cause for concern. He was worried that we might peak too early and be played out when we got back to New York. Although he tried not to show it, it was obvious that our farewell performance was extremely important to him. He wanted us to go out in style.

"Pace yourselves," he lectured us. "We've got forty cities and six thousand miles to go. Don't blow yourselves out."

Ellen joined the tour in Providence, coming up on the midnight train from New York. Polly and Harry and I hurried over to Union Station after our last set at the Starlite Roof. Even at that late hour, the station was jammed with men and women in uniform. We went past a Red Cross canteen that was serving coffee and doughnuts to servicemen. Ellen, wearing a floppy hat and a tailored suit with padded shoulders, was the first one off the train.

"Yoo-hoo, over here, Ellen!" Polly called, and we pushed through the crowd.

Ellen gave Polly a warm hug. "How are you, dear?" she said, and to Harry and me, "And how are my favorite wise guys?"

"I can't believe Gene finally let you out of that office," Polly said.

"It's like a holiday," Ellen said. "I haven't been on a road tour since — well, never mind when."

Harry reached for her luggage and turned on the charm. "Ellen, you look very chic, very —" He snapped his fingers at me. "Skeeter, a well-turned phrase, if you will."

"Very Main Line Philadelphia," I said.

"Exactly."

Ellen looked anxiously up and down the platform. "Where's Gene?" she said.

"He and Gus are still at the Starlite Roof," I said. "He was planning to meet you, but the management tried to gyp us on the gross."

"Who caught them?" Ellen asked.

"Basil," Polly said. "Who else?"

"That Basil," Ellen said. "He'd run the band, if we let him."

Ellen Bowe was the most popular and respected member of Gene's musical organization, which included, besides the band, a sheet music company. She'd been with Gene since her graduation from Bryn Mawr. At first, she had worked as a vocalist, then switched to office manager and girl Friday, exerting a gentle influence that tempered Gene's aloofness.

"Well," she sighed, "I hope Gus remembered to reserve a room for me."

"You're staying with me, Ellen," Polly said. "We've never had another girl on the tour before, and I'm sick of being one of the boys."

"You must be exhausted," Ellen said. "I'd forgotten how primitive the road can be, living out of a suitcase and a bus."

"Was it that way when you traveled with the band?" Polly asked her.

"Worse," Ellen replied. "You wouldn't believe some of the things we went through."

We stopped at the Union Station coffee shop for sandwiches. Ellen hadn't eaten; the diner on her train had run out of food. And as we ate, she talked of her years with Gene's first band, of dreary one-nighters in towns she'd never heard of — Pottsville, Ashtabula, Streator — using pickup musicians when the money ran out, and never knowing if they'd be sober, or if they'd show up at all.

"It's funny," she said, smiling softly. "Those were hard years. My diamond was in and out of hock a dozen times. We ate in greasy spoons and slept in cars, and a broken saxophone was a catastrophe. But when you look back, it all seems so lovely."

"What made you stick it out, Ellen?" I asked her. "You must've had lots of other opportunities."

"Gene," she admitted frankly. "I had a crush on him from the start. He was so dedicated, so sweet."

"Sweet?" Polly giggled. "I can't imagine his being sweet. Smooth, maybe, or overpowering, but *sweet*?"

"He's really a very remarkable man, Polly," Ellen said. "Oh, I know people say he's a cold fish, that all he cares about is making the cash register ring. But deep down, he's a very sensitive and compassionate man. He's been very concerned about you, you know. He thinks you ought to consider a nightclub act."

"There's been talk of some of us forming a combo," Polly said.

"Wonderful!" Ellen said. "A trio?"

"A quintet," Polly said. "Skeets and Harry, Augie and Buddy."

"And you for vocals?"

"That's the general idea," Polly said. "But I'm not sure what I want to do. Besides, it's all sort of a pipe dream. Money."

Ellen nodded her head slowly. "Yes, it would be expensive," she said. "Gene lost twenty thousand on his first band. But if you succeed, it's more than worth it."

"And if we don't?" Polly said.

"Assume that you will," Ellen said. "You've got to be optimistic."

I asked Ellen if she would help me figure out cost estimates for a combo.

"I told the guys I'd come up with a tentative budget."

"I'd be glad to, Skeets," she said. "How would you raise the money?"

"Pool what money we've got, I guess, and borrow the rest. Maybe a bank loan."

"And what would we put up for collateral?" Polly said. "A dream?"

Ellen had brought along our mail, which she passed out at breakfast. Gus hadn't heard from his son since Christmas, and there was still no word.

"Kids," he said. "No consideration. He and Harry are peas in a pod. Not a care in the world."

"I wouldn't worry, Gus," Ellen said. "Mail from the war zones takes ages. You'll probably get a dozen letters all at once."

There was a letter for me from Princess Anne, one for Harry from his draft board, and one for Polly from St. Mary's.

"You haven't been reclassified, have you?" I asked Harry.

He winked and made a circle with his thumb and forefinger. "No strain, Skeeter," he said. "My deferment's good as gold."

41

My letter was from my father. I started to open it, then hesitated; it would simply be a continuation of the old argument. When was I going to come to my senses? An itinerant dance orchestra was no career. He wasn't getting any younger, and with my sisters married and moved away, who would take over the lumberyard?

"Aren't you going to read your mail, Skeets?" Polly asked me as we left the hotel.

"I'll read it on the bus," I said, and slipped the letter into a pocket.

But I didn't intend to read it on the bus, or in Boston, perhaps not till the tour was over. That was one of the advantages of the road — responsibilities could be put off. The truth was, I wasn't ready to cope with the future, beyond some plan that would keep me close to Polly.

Originally, Harry and I had considered the band merely a phase in our musical development. Our futures, we were convinced, lay in classical music. At Juilliard, Harry had seemed destined for a career as a concert pianist, while I aspired to a chair in a major symphony orchestra, preferably the Boston Symphony, which was conducted by Serge Koussevitzky.

When Gene first told us that he had applied for a commission in the army, I had written to the Boston Symphony, as well as to a few lesser choices. Only the New York Philharmonic had replied. They would be auditioning in August for chairs that would be empty in September. It was a good possibility, but now I was undecided, realizing that the band had given a new direction to my musical interests — and to Harry's.

42

Harry obviously lacked the personal discipline necessary for a concert career. Jazz, however, offered him
full expression of his inventive talents. Harry could
take a simple theme — a nursery tune or a hymn — and
weave seemingly endless variations on it. He was the
inspiration for the piano concerto I was working on,
which was simply a series of variations on a Scott Jop-
lin ragtime theme, constructed in the manner of Gersh-
win's *Concerto in F*. I had wild fantasies of Harry's
performing it one day in Carnegie Hall, perhaps with
Koussevitzky conducting. There would be a standing
ovation, and the audience would cry, "Composer! Composer!"

Polly figured in that dream, too, standing by my side
as I bowed to the audience. Polly figured in all of my
dreams, romantically, erotically, improbably. On the
trip up to Boston that morning, I caught myself sneaking glances at her. A riot of thoughts rushed through
my head — of Polly's becoming a great success in our
combo, of her being offered a movie contract, and of
me as her trusted friend and confidant, guiding her
career —

"*Skeets!*" Polly's voice jarred me back to reality.
"What on earth are you staring at?"

"Sorry," I mumbled. "I was just thinking."

She frowned. "About what?"

"About Boston." I could feel my cheeks burning.
"Why don't you get one of the Mellow Birds to take
you out? You could triple-date with Harry and me."

"No, thank you," she said. "I couldn't put up with
Sarah's airs for a whole evening. Anyhow, Gus and

Ellen and I are going to dinner and a show. Basil's coming with us."

Two days later, in the lobby of the Copley Plaza Hotel, with an evening of leisure stretching out before us, Harry and I ran into Polly as we were leaving to pick up our dates. She looked very ladylike, in heels and a dress of dotted Swiss, with a knit shawl borrowed from Ellen thrown over her shoulders. And suddenly I wished Harry hadn't suckered me into the double-date. It would be so much nicer to spend the evening with Polly and the others.

"Are you sure you won't change your mind and come with us?" I asked her.

"I'd just cramp your style, Skeets," she said. "Call me when you get back. We'll talk."

Harry and I crossed the lobby and went out into Copley Square. Harry drew a deep breath and threw an arm around me.

"Ah, Boston in the spring!" He took Sarah's ring from his pocket and polished it on his sleeve. "Skeeter, there are times when the world is your oyster, and this is one of them."

We piled into a waiting cab.

"North Station, my good man," Harry instructed the driver. "And don't spare the horses."

·4·
A *Largo* in Copley Square

But the world wasn't Harry's oyster, at least not that night. Four hours later, we were standing in front of the Parker House hotel, arguing — Harry and I, Sarah's roommate, who regarded me as some kind of worm, and Sarah, who was furious.

"We could've gone to a fraternity dance in Cambridge," she said. "I wish now that we had."

Harry threw up his arms in exasperation and hailed a cab.

"There's no point in your coming along, Skeeter," he said. "I'll see you back at the hotel."

Harry was unfailingly chivalrous. He would see them back to the campus, in Beverly Farms, and be stuck out there half the night. Sarah, a small girl with a snappish way about her, could be a brat when she wanted.

Almost from the begining, the evening had fallen apart. Harry had suggested dinner at an Italian place, but Sarah had insisted on the Ritz. Then I had suggested drinks at a Dixieland club, but Sarah had insisted on the Parker House, which meant no drinks (the girls didn't have fake IDs). And all evening, Sarah kept needling Harry about the band.

"It's so ridiculous, Harry. You could go to Harvard Law and join your father's firm."

"But I'm not interested in law, Sarah."

"But a musician, Harry. It's so — ordinary."

I felt like sinking into my chair; my date, however, seemed indifferent to Harry's embarrassment.

The cab drove off toward North Station, and I started back to the hotel. It disturbed me, the way Harry let Sarah walk all over him. With everyone else, he was the most self-assured person I'd ever known.

Back at the Copley, I looked for Augie and Buddy in the bar, but they'd gone on a tour of the jazz joints and weren't back yet. I rang Polly's room on the house phone in the lobby. No answer. It was a heck of a night to be stuck alone. I went up to the eighth-floor room that Harry and I were sharing. It was a bright night, and the moonlight came in the window. I left the lights off and stretched out on my bed. In a moment, there was a rap on the door. It was Polly.

"I called to you in the lobby," she said. "We were just coming in."

"Was it a good movie?"

"Yes, lovely." She leaned against the door to catch her breath. "We saw *Mrs. Miniver*. Gene came with us. He held Ellen's hand during the sad parts."

"Really? Maybe we'll be hearing wedding bells after all."

"I hope so. I'd hate to see him go off to war with no one to kiss him good-bye."

I started to turn on the lights.

"No, leave them off, Skeets. I like it like this. Have you got anything to drink?"

"Harry's got some gin and grapefruit juice."

"Ugh, how can he drink that stuff? No, I just want some ginger ale or something."

"Would you settle for ice water?"

"Yes, that would be fine." She slipped off her coat. "How come you're back so early?"

"Harry and Sarah had a fight."

"Over what?"

"The usual. Harry's being a musician."

"Not again. Sarah's going to lose him if she doesn't watch out."

"I think she already has." I filled a glass from the ice-water tap in the bathroom. "He took them back to school, but he was pretty sore."

"Well — it's no great loss, if you ask me. Sarah's a pill, but I feel sorry for Harry. They've gone together for so long, and he'd bought the ring and all."

There was a small settee and a coffee table next to the window. Polly sipped her water and set the glass on the table. "Tell me about tonight," she said. "What was your date like?"

I slouched into a corner of the settee. "Too arty," I said, "and too tall."

She sat down next to me. "Honestly, Skeets, you've got to stop being so shy about girls. You're not that short, and you're as nice looking as any other boy. But you've got to assert yourself."

We sat in silence for a moment. Then I asked her the

question that had been worrying me for two weeks. "Polly — why did you faint on the bus?"

She kicked off her shoes and tucked her legs up under her. "Darn you, Skeets. You would have to bring that up."

"But you promised you'd tell me."

"You won't say anything to Gus?"

"I haven't yet, have I?"

"All right. I've got a murmur. A defect in my heart."

"Is it serious?"

"Not really. So long as I eat the right foods and get plenty of rest."

"Is that why you're always napping between shows?"

"Yes. I'm supposed to avoid overexerting myself."

"But you were okay till that night on the bus."

She shook her head. "No, it's happened before. I get spells when I feel weak and fluttery. But they've always come when I've been alone."

"How come they let you join the band in the first place?"

"I didn't know anything was wrong till that time I went to the doctor when I had laryngitis. If Gene finds out, he'll probably put me on the first train to Saint Mary's."

"But you're over eighteen now. You wouldn't have to go back if you didn't want to."

"I know. But I'm not sure I could make it on my own. I've been thinking about going to college, but I'm not sure I could handle even that."

"College? But what about your career?"

"Singing isn't that important to me, Skeets. It was just a way out of the orphanage."

"College would be expensive. Could you swing it?"

"I think so. I've been making eighty a week. Gus gives me enough to live on and banks the rest. I must have a thousand dollars in my account."

"Then what's the problem?"

"I don't know." She twisted around and tilted her head against my shoulder. "Sometimes I think going back to Saint Mary's would be the best thing for me. For a while, anyway. Sister Angela wrote that they'll give me a job if I want it. Teaching choir. I'd have a private room and could come and go as I pleased."

"What's it like there, Polly?"

"Saint Mary's? It's out in the country, like a campus. It's very nice, really, but you have to sleep in a dormitory and wear hand-me-down clothes. You can't have pets or anything, and I've always wanted a dog. We didn't even have a phonograph. Sister Angela never had enough money to buy us one."

"What do you remember about your home before Saint Mary's?"

"Nothing. I was only three weeks old when I was brought there. I was illegitimate. Sister Angela never told me so, but you sense things. Nearly all the kids were. The farmers used to call us bastards —"

The word jolted me. I'd heard it often enough, but it seemed ugly when applied to Polly.

"I never knew what it meant till sixth grade, and then I started wondering about my parents. My mother, mostly. At first, I imagined all kinds of romantic things about her, and then I began to resent her for abandoning me."

"But maybe she couldn't help it," I said. "Maybe she got into trouble and had nowhere to turn."

"Maybe," Polly said, a tightness coming into her voice. "But I still can't forgive her. Sometimes I —"

Her lips were trembling. Suddenly she slipped into my arms.

"Hold me, Skeets," she whispered. "Just hold me."

And in that moment, with Polly pressing tightly against me and the moonlight coming in the window — I ached for her. We sat that way for several minutes. Polly seemed to have fallen asleep. Then a key rattled in the door, and Harry flipped on the lights.

"Well, well." He glanced over at us and raised an eyebrow. "Should I send out announcements?"

"Oh, Harry." Polly sat up and smoothed her dress. "Didn't you go out to Beverly Farms with Sarah?"

Harry shook his head and made a thumbs-down gesture. I could tell that he'd had a few drinks.

"She jilted me. Can you beat that?" He mimicked Sarah's voice. " 'You're all mixed up, Harry. You've got to try to find yourself.' I was so disgusted, I got off the train at Salem and took a cab back."

"Poor Harry," Polly said.

He proceeded straight to the bottle of gin that was on the dresser.

"This calls for a salty dog," he said as he mixed the gin with grapefruit juice. "It isn't every day that a guy gets jilted."

He was on his second drink when there was another rap on the door. It was Augie and Buddy returning from their night on the town.

"The springtime boys!" Harry called to them. "Just in time fer a salty dog."

"Those things'll knock you on your keister," Augie said, sitting down on Harry's bed. "We'll stick to beer."

"We don't have any beer," I said.

"Then we'll get some," Buddy said.

He called room service and ordered beer, pretzels, and some ginger ale for Polly. Soon we had a fine party going.

"Hey, you know something?" Augie said. "We heard some fine combos tonight, and none of them had a vibraphone."

"So?" I said.

"So it's an idea for our combo," he said. "Something that'd make us different. Not on every number, just special ones."

"And where d'we find a guy that plays vibes?" Harry said, mixing another drink.

"I can play 'em," Augie said.

"Seriously, Augie?" Polly said.

"Sure, I can play anything that gets hit," Augie said. "A guy back in Elkhart taught me vibes when I was still in high school."

"And who plays drums," Harry asked him, "while yer playin' vibes?"

"I thought of that, too," he said. "Basil's coming along real well. He could fill in on drums when I'm on vibes."

"Basil!" Polly broke into laughter. "I figured he'd worm his way in."

"But it's really very practical," Augie said. "We'd be

getting a band boy and a drummer for the price of one."

"The only practical thing about this whole scheme," Polly said, "is the fact that you don't have any money."

Buddy nudged her and grinned. "Polly baby," he said, "if you're gonna eam-dray, eam-dray ig-bay."

"Uts-nay," Polly retorted.

We talked till two o'clock, and even Polly found herself finally succumbing to the dream.

"On some of the vocals, the four of you could back me up as a little glee club," she said. "Not in harmony, but just singing melody."

When the party finally broke up, Harry polished off all that remained of the gin and grapefruit juice.

"Aren't you hitting that stuff kind of hard?" I said to him.

He reached unsteadily for his pajamas. "Jus' a li'l nightcap, Skeeter," he said. "After all, it's been a big night fer me."

"Don't worry, Harry. Sarah will come to her senses."

"Who cares?" he said, shrugging. "There're plenty other fish in the sea. I may even give Polly a tumble."

"Don't, Harry," I said. "She's going through a difficult time. It'd only complicate things."

"Well — we'll see." He finished his drink and grabbed hold of a bedpost. "Oh-oh," he said wanly. "Room's gettin' wobbly." He was asleep the moment his head touched the pillow.

I tossed restlessly that night. I could almost feel Polly's softness and smell her fragrance. And as I lay awake, a brooding melody kept running through my

mind. The *largo* of some forgotten symphony, I thought
— or was it? I slipped out of bed, turned on a lamp,
and rummaged in my suitcase for my music paper and
World's Fair pen. I sat crosslegged on the floor and
started humming, pausing occasionally to jot down the
notes. I worked long into the night, expanding the
theme in delicate variations. When my head began to
nod, I put my music aside and went to the window. A
silvery mist hung over a church across the square. A
taxi pulled up at the hotel, then drove off into the lonely
night. If only it could be put to music, I thought —
Boston and the road and the melancholy feeling of a
hotel room at night. And Polly — to put Polly to music,
with flutes and strings and the soft tinkling of chimes.

If only there would be enough time . . .

·5·
Trouble in Detroit

In Boston, Basil had made two capital expenditures: a new pair of socks — argyles, in a bright plaid — and a portable radio, which he bought at a pawnshop.

The socks were a failure. "Good grief!" Ellen exclaimed. "They're so loud, they practically shout."

The radio, however, was a great success, and Basil soon had a problem with the many requests for programs. We all looked forward to Jack Benny's program, whenever our schedule would allow us to listen. Polly's favorite was *Lux Radio Theater*, which featured Hollywood stars. When we played stage shows at the big movie houses, Basil would tune in the radio backstage to ease our boredom between shows.

"Keep it low," Gus cautioned him. "The audience will hear that damn thing if it's too loud."

One night, between shows at the Rialto in Pittsburgh, Basil was tuning in *The Shadow*, a mystery, and mistakenly had the volume up full. In a tender moment of the film, as George Brent was about to embrace Bette Davis, *"Who knows what evil lurks in the hearts of men?"* suddenly blared out, so loud it filled the theater. The audience roared, but Gus didn't think it was funny.

"No more radio backstage!" he decreed. "You wanna get us all canned?"

Basil's preference was for the news commentators, several of whom had stories about Gene's joining the army.

"You're pretty big stuff when Raymond Gram Swing does a story on you," he said, beaming with pride. "Wait'll I tell Gene."

As we left New England and worked our way west, there was little talk of our combo. Our enthusiasm in Boston, I concluded, had been induced by the drinks. Polly once again seemed indifferent to the idea, and all Harry had to say was that Augie's idea of a vibraphone was dumb.

"Who ever heard of a drummer doubling on vibes?" he said. "It's like a trombonist doubling on an oboe."

"Harry!" Basil protested. "If Augie doesn't play vibes, I don't get to play drums."

"You wouldn't get a chance, anyway," Harry said. "Augie doesn't own any drums."

If Harry was planning to give Polly a rush, there was no indication of it. I noticed him staring at her a few times, but nothing more. He had been spending most of his free time drinking with the party boys in the trumpet section, whose after-hours escapades gave Gus his biggest headache. In Youngstown, Harry nearly got into a fight with a marine sergeant who called him a draft dodger. And in Canton, he lost his shirt in an all-night poker game and nearly missed the bus.

"That was cutting it pretty close, Harry," I said. "Gus is really burned."

"So let him burn," he retorted. "I'm fed up with this chicken outfit."

"Aw, come on, Harry. You'll get canned if you miss the bus."

"So I get canned. So what? We're all going to get canned when we get back to New York. Now leave me alone, will you?"

Polly blamed his souring attitude on the split with Sarah, but I had a feeling that it went deeper than that. The tour was having an unsettling effect on all of us. It was our first trip back to the Middle West since that wintry night in the Galesburg depot, and the impact of the war was awesome — the glare of factories at night, the constant movement of troop trains, the blue stars that hung in the windows of nearly every house, signifying a member of the family in service. The cities were filled with pleasure-seeking war workers and men in uniform. When we played the clubs, there was a great deal of drunkenness. The ballrooms were more restrained. Shy young girls danced with shy young soldiers, and their lives were changed because of it.

"I just love the ballrooms," Polly said. "You can see so many romances blooming, and our music is a part of it."

Yet even the tender moments were clouded by the war. Basil kept us posted on the latest developments. The only really good news was Colonel Jimmy Doolittle's B-25 raid on Tokyo, planned at President Roosevelt's secret retreat identified as "Shangri-la." Everyone suspected it was launched from an American aircraft carrier.

"That'll teach those Japs to mess with us," Basil said.

But the other side of the coin was grim. Russia appeared doomed, and German U-boats were torpedoing our convoys within periscope range of Norfolk. Oil slicks and debris washed up on the beaches. I worried about my parents. Princess Anne was only a few miles south of Norfolk. I still hadn't opened that letter from my father. I would read it when we got to Detroit, I resolved, and write him a long, friendly reply.

But in Detroit, there was scarcely time to think. Two military dates, a war bond rally, and a one-nighter at Eastwood Gardens. We were tired and edgy. Harry was nursing a hangover, and Gus, who still hadn't heard from his son, had come down with a touch of bursitis. When we arrived at the Book-Cadillac Hotel, we were immediately whisked off to a breakfast date at a nearby naval air station.

"They want us there early," Gus said. "They've got a presentation for Polly."

Harry groaned. "What is it this time?" he said. "The girl they'd most like to come home to?"

"No," Gus said. "The girl they'd most like to bail out with. Now hustle your bustle, wise guy. There's a war on, in case you haven't heard."

We were nervous about Detroit. Tanks and guns poured from its factories, but there was unrest in the air, a tension that you could almost feel. Thousands of workers, most of them from the South and many of them black, had flocked to the city for jobs in war plants.

At Eastwood Gardens, a garish ballroom set amid the root-beer glitter of an amusement park, we had another record-breaking crowd — predominantly white, but with a sprinkling of blacks. Toward the end of our second set, we noticed some commotion on the floor. A large group of whites — servicemen and boys of high-school age — had gathered off to one side. Then quickly, in threes and fours, they fanned out among the dancers and began forcing the blacks toward a fire exit, which someone had thrown open.

"I don't believe it!" Augie exclaimed. "They're kicking the black kids out!"

We were doing "Blue Champagne," and I had a clarinet solo at the stage mike. I was so upset I squeaked a note, and the whole band faltered. Gene came up behind me.

"Take over, Skeets," he ordered me. "Skip the intermission and go straight into the next set. Just keep them playing."

He hurried offstage. We finished the number, and I quickly gave the beat for "American Patrol." It was the first time I'd ever led a band, and I was frightened and confused, convinced that a riot was about to break out. Gene had gone around to the fire exit. I could see him talking to the black couples, who had gathered in a tight circle. Two policemen appeared, then the manager of the ballroom. Flashbulbs were popping. Gene raised an arm and gestured angrily to the manager. This can't be happening, I thought — and then felt a hand on my shoulder.

"The bus is all set, Skeets." It was Gus, who had

come out from the wings to give me instructions. "If things get hot, grab the instruments and make a run for it."

Three sailors were dragging a brown-skinned boy in a plaid jacket from the floor. He looked up at me as though appealing for help. Our eyes met briefly and held, and in that moment I felt guilty and ashamed, for I was from Virginia, where black people were forbidden to drink from the same fountains as whites.

"Why the hell doesn't Old Stone Face do something?" I heard Harry mutter at the piano.

And then suddenly, the exit door slammed shut, and it was over. We went into "Stardust" as though nothing had happened. After the last set, Gus wasted little time in getting us out of there. On the bus, he counted heads to make sure we'd all made it. Only Augie and Buddy were missing.

"They spotted some choice girls," Basil said. "They'll probably make a night of it."

"Then everyone's present or accounted for," Gus said.

"Everyone but Chicken Little," Harry said.

"And what's that supposed to mean, wise guy?"

"You know damn well what it means, Gus. You saw Gene beat it away from the ballroom in a cab. He's afraid to ride with us. He should've stood up and been counted tonight, and he knows it."

Harry wasn't being entirely fair. One of Ellen's college friends was giving a party in Grosse Pointe, and she and Gene had taken a taxi from Eastwood Gardens. Still, we were all thinking the same thing. Gene should have acted in some way.

"Harry's right, Gus," Polly said. "There must've been something Gene could have done."

"Like what?" Gus said. "Make a speech? He's a musician, not a politician."

"Excuses, excuses," Harry persisted. "They paid their admission the same as the white kids."

"Since when did you get religion, wise guy? When we played the Blue Room, the crowd was white as snow, and there wasn't a peep out of you."

"New Orleans is different," Harry said.

"Oh, yeah?" Gus said. "Well, tell me, why is it right in New Orleans and wrong in Detroit?"

Gus had us. We had played every major club and ballroom in the South, and a black person couldn't have bought a ticket for a thousand dollars. It was the way things were, and we had accepted the arrangement uncritically.

"They've got laws down South," Harry said lamely. "It's hard to do anything when they've got laws."

Back at the hotel, the early edition of the *Free Press* had come in. Basil glanced at the front page and let out a little yell.

"Look!" he cried.

BANDLEADER INTRUDES INTO BALLROOM FRACAS

"Why didn't you tell us he'd done something, Gus?" Polly said.

"I didn't know," Gus said. "He stormed out of there so fast, I didn't have two words with him."

Polly scanned the story hurriedly. There was a photograph of Gene with his arm raised — the same scene that I'd observed from the bandstand, with the policemen, the manager, and the black couples huddled in a circle. "It says the manager refused to refund their admission, but that Gene made it good out of his own pocket. Isn't that wonderful?"

Then her eyes grew wide.

"I don't believe it," she said. "They're criticizing him for what he did. Listen to this. 'Police said they deplore Markham's precipitous action.' "

"That's the way it is, kitten," Gus said. "Even the newspapers give blacks a raw deal."

Polly bought two copies of the paper.

"Well, I don't care what they say," she said. "I'm proud of Gene. I'm going to send a copy to Sister Angela. There're a lot of black kids at Saint Mary's, and they'll be proud, too."

It wasn't until we were walking to the elevator that we discovered that Harry had wandered off.

"Not again," Polly said. "He won't be able to see the keys tomorrow. What time does the bus leave, Gus?"

"Seven-fifteen sharp."

"I'll call your room at six, Skeets," she said to me. "You'll probably have to blast him out of bed."

✦   ✦

Polly called our room earlier than she had anticipated. It seemed I'd barely fallen asleep when the phone rang. I fumbled for it in the dark.

"Has Harry come in yet?"

"Just a second." I turned on the light. Harry's bed hadn't been slept in. "No."

"I was afraid of that," she said. "Ellen thought she saw him walking down toward the river when she and Gene were coming back from Grosse Point. Where on earth could he be?"

"Some bar, probably," I said, yawning.

"At this hour? The bars close at two o'clock in Michigan."

"Jiffy's is still open." I looked at my watch; it was three-thirty. "I'd better go get him."

"I'll go with you."

"No, Polly. You need your sleep. I'll call Augie and Buddy."

"They're not back yet. What if he's passed out or something?"

"Okay." I yawned again. "I'll meet you in the lobby in ten minutes."

The Detroit River was only a few blocks from the hotel. Jiffy's, an all-night jazz joint, was in the basement of a building opposite the railroad yards that lined the riverfront.

"The door is around in the alley," I said to Polly.

"I've never been to a place like this before," she said. "Do you have to know someone?"

"Not here," I said. "Jiffy used to be a cop."

A blare of music hit us like a shock wave as a man in a pin-striped suit let us in.

"We're with Gene Markham's band," I told him.

"Okay, buddy," he said. "There's a two-buck cover charge, but that includes the lady."

Harry and I had been to Jiffy's twice before. It was

a dive, a crowded, smoky, ill-smelling place, with sawdust on the floor and utility pipes hanging from the ceiling. But the acoustics were superb, and once the jam sessions started, you hated to leave.

"There's Harry," Polly said, standing on her toes to see above the crowd. "At the piano."

A small combo was doing a furious version of "Ida," Dixieland style — trumpet, trombone, clarinet, string bass, drums, and Harry, in shirtsleeves, at a battered upright piano. Other musicians wandered in and out of the group. When the perspiring clarinetist paused to wipe his brow, a Negro in a tan jacket leaped up from one of the tables, blowing a wild alto sax. When Harry spotted us and left the stand, someone else slipped in at the piano, without missing a beat.

"Skeeter! Pols!" Harry hollered above the noise, pointing to an empty table across the room. "Over here!"

"He looks awful," Polly said. "It's just drinking, isn't it, Skeets? It isn't marijuana or something?"

"Oh, no," I replied. "Harry doesn't fool around with that stuff."

Harry drew a big round of applause from the crowd, which he acknowledged with a wave and a grin. I couldn't help admiring the ease with which he moved through life, but for the first time, I realized that he was on a binge that was careening out of control. His eyes were red, his clothes rumpled, and he walked with a slight list. It was as though something had gone haywire inside him, something that none of us understood. He greeted us as though he owned the joint.

"Great crowd t'night, kiddies," he said. "See that

guy on sax, Pols? He plays with Count Basie. They're openin' t'morrow at the River Inn."

We squeezed around a tiny table that was scarred with cigarette burns. "A round of drinks, sweetie," Harry called to a passing waitress, and to me, "They've still got some imported Scotch, Skeeter. Fantastic stuff."

"Imported Scotch?" I said. "For crying out loud, Harry, what're you using for money?"

"Money?" He grinned stupidly and pulled some crumpled bills from his pocket. "Hell, ah'm rollin' in the stuff."

A little stub fell from among the bills. Polly picked it up. It was a pawn ticket.

"Harry, you didn't," she said. "You haven't even paid for that ring, and now you've gone and hocked it."

Harry shrugged. "No sweat, Pols," he said. "Easy come, easy go."

The waitress arrived with three highballs.

"Take them back," Polly ordered her. "Skeets, go find Harry's coat. We've got a bus to catch."

Harry grabbed the waitress's arm. "Leave 'em, sweetie," he said, wagging a finger under Polly's nose. "Maybe you've got a bus t'catch, Pols, but this kid don't — doesn't."

"What are you talking about, Harry?" I said. "You're not quitting the band?"

"Brilliant d'duction, Skeeter. Not only am I quittin' the damn band, I'm quittin' your dumb idea of a combo, and I'm quittin' the whole damn music business. Sarah was right. It's a lousy way t' make a livin'. How many guys really make it big? You c'n count 'em on one hand.

You beat your brains out and end up band director of some Podunk high school. Big deal."

"But you can't quit now, Harry," I argued. "It wouldn't be fair to Gene or Gus."

"Fair t' Gus?" Harry gave a scornful laugh. "Ha! When's he ever been fair t' me?"

And he launched into a bleary recitation of his grievances — Gene's refusal to let the band swing, Gus's Cub Scout regulations, Weintraub's column in *Metronome*. I listened patiently and then made a serious tactical error. I was so upset that I forgot we were dealing with a drunk.

"You don't know what you're saying, Harry." I took him by the arm. "Come on, you'll feel better when you've had some sleep."

"God damn it, Skeeter! Take your hands off me!"

He jerked his arm away so abruptly that his hand grazed my face and knocked my glasses off. My vision was a blur without them. I got down on my hands and knees and felt for them in the sawdust. "Damn you, Harry," I said. "Why'd you go and do that?"

"You asked for it, squirt. Now scram. Both of you."

People at the other tables were staring at us. Polly found my glasses. They were unbroken. I brushed off the sawdust and put them on. A man with a thick neck and scarred chin was approaching our table from the bar. It was Jiffy.

"What's the trouble, sport?" he asked Harry.

"Couple o' moochers, Jiff. Can't a guy have any privacy?"

Jiffy turned to Polly and me.

"Beat it, bud," he said, jerking a thumb toward the door. "You too, tootsie."

"Don't 'tootsie' me," Polly snapped. She brushed him aside and leaned down over Harry, who had already finished two of the drinks.

"Harry, listen to me," she said. "We all love you. If you want to quit music — okay, quit. But not till we get back to New York. Don't let your friends down." She gave Jiffy a dirty look and took my hand. "Come on, Skeets."

We started for the door.

"The bus leaves at seven-fifteen, Harry," she called back. "We'll have your bags packed."

Outside, the morning air was cool and fresh. Polly sat down on a packing crate in the alley.

"Let's rest for a minute, Skeets," she said. "I feel drained."

"You should have stayed at the hotel," I said. "You're pushing yourself into one of your spells."

"So I'll have a spell," she said. "What business is it of yours? It's *my* heart, and if I —" She broke off. "Oh, darn, now even *we're* bickering."

"It's all right, Polly. We've all been edgy."

"No, it's not all right," she said. "What's happening to us? We're not the same anymore. Nothing's the same."

I thought of our last night at the Emerald Room, the night we voted on the tour.

"Maybe the tour was a mistake," I said. "Maybe we should have stayed in New York."

"Maybe," Polly said. "Then again, maybe not. Does this place have a phone?"

"Sure. Why?"

"I'll call when we get back to the hotel. Do you think we could talk Gus into holding the bus for Harry?"

"I doubt it," I replied. "But what can we lose?"

It was dawn when we got back to the hotel. Augie and Buddy were just returning from their excursion, looking surprisingly rested.

"I hope you made out," I said.

Buddy smiled complacently. "It's bad manners," he said, "to kiss and tell."

"Don't let him kid you," Augie said. "It was a goose egg. We spent the whole night riding around in a streetcar."

At breakfast, we told them about Harry.

"Looks like the quintet has been reduced to a quartet," Augie said.

"A trio, you mean," Polly said. "I never said I was definitely in."

The bus pulled up in front of the Book-Cadillac at 7:00. Buddy and Augie lugged Harry's bags out to the curb. If he didn't show up, we'd made arrangements to leave them with the room clerk. Polly had phoned Jiffy's, but with disappointing results.

"That place is a madhouse," she said. "I don't think anyone understood what I was talking about."

We hadn't talked to Gus yet; Polly was hoping it wouldn't be necessary. Gene and Ellen were already in the bus, working on the Eastwood Gardens receipts. The rest of the band drifted out from the coffee shop. Gus stood at the door of the bus, checking them off. When they were all aboard, we took him aside and told him about Harry.

"If you could just wait a few minutes," Polly begged him. "I'm sure he'll show up."

"That's not good enough, kitten," Gus said. "You know the rules. The bus leaves on time. Period. Stragglers can look for another job."

"But what'll we do for a pianist?" I said.

"Piano players are a dime a dozen," Gus said. "We can call the union and have one over here in ten seconds."

"Not like Harry," I said.

"Maybe not," he said. "But let me give you the first rule of life, Skeets. Talent doesn't mean a thing if you don't show up. And the second rule is, there are no exceptions to the first rule. Sorry."

I looked at my watch. It was 7:12.

"Well —" I said to Polly. "We'd better take Harry's bags inside."

"Not yet, Skeets. Look."

Gus had gone around to the rear of the bus and was kicking at one of the tires.

"Hey, buddy," he called to the driver. "This tire doesn't look so hot."

The driver climbed out and inspected the tire.

"Looks okay to me," he said.

"Oh, yeah?" Gus said. "That valve stem won't last fifty miles. Run in to the hotel garage and get the mechanic."

Gene heard the commotion and opened a window. "What's the delay, Gus?"

"Tire trouble. The mechanic's gonna check it out. Shouldn't take more than ten minutes."

Gene closed the window, apparently satisfied. I breathed a sigh of relief.

"You'd better be right about Harry," I said to Polly. "Gus is really sticking his neck out."

The minutes ticked by with no sign of Harry. I kept glancing at my watch. At 7:25 the driver reappeared, accompanied by a man carrying a toolbox.

"It's no use, Polly," I said. "Harry's really blown it this time."

Basil started to pick up Harry's bags. "Should I take them in to the room clerk, Polly?" he asked.

"I guess so, Basil," she said. "Poor Harry."

But at that moment, a taxi rattled to a stop behind the bus. A black man got out. A false alarm, I thought — and then recognized him as the sax player we'd seen at Jiffy's, the one with Count Basie's band. He reached back into the cab and dragged Harry out.

"Quick, Basil," Polly said. "Get his bags aboard."

She called to Augie and Buddy, who piled out of the bus and took custody of Harry.

"Put him in his usual seat," she told them. "I'll make a bed for him."

"Keep him nice and warm, miss," the sax player said. "You don't want his fingers to get stiff. That boy can really stroke the ivories."

Gus scowled. "Looks like he can stroke the booze pretty good, too," he said.

The black man laughed. "For a fact," he said. "But a boy like that's worth a little trouble."

Gus extended a hand. "Gus Oshinsky," he said. "Thanks for your help, pal."

"Chummy Hines," the man said. "You boys headin' west?"

"Yeah," Gus said. "Dallas, Seattle, L.A., the works."

"We're on our way back," Chummy Hines said. "Man, it's wild out there on the coast. Everybody makin' big money in the aircraft plants and livin' it up. Well, lots of luck to you."

It was always nice to run into sidemen from other bands on the road. But there was something special about this encounter. It seemed to cancel out the unpleasantness at Eastwood Gardens.

"Gus, we need some towels or something." Polly stuck her head out the bus door. "He's throwing up."

Gus bit down hard on his cigar.

"A regular nursery," he muttered. "I should've stuck with the carnival."

Finally, the bus started moving. Our next date was at an army camp in the western part of the state, followed by a one-nighter in Kalamazoo, which would include a lot of fast numbers for a jitterbug contest. We had four hours, five at the most, to get Harry in shape. As we wound through downtown Detroit, Polly and I got pillows and blankets from the luggage rack and tried to get some sleep.

The road was beginning to take its toll.

·6·
Reaching for It

I don't know how Harry survived the next few days. His hands trembled, and solid foods made him vomit. Gene had tactfully turned his head during the scene in the bus, preferring to let Gus handle it. Gene always knew what was going on. He proceeded to deal with Harry in his own way, scheduling difficult arrangements, calling for cuts or repeats without warning, lengthening Harry's solos. It was his method of teaching you a lesson, applying the pressure when you were least able to take it, and it seldom failed.

But through it all, Harry performed superbly, never hitting a sour note or missing a cue.

"I've disconnected my brain," he said in Grand Rapids. "My fingers are doing my thinking."

Curiously, Harry's problems seemed to draw him closer to Polly. As we left Michigan and began to swing through Indiana, she fussed over him so much, I worried that she might start sitting next to him in the bus. It was just her "wounded bird" tendencies, I told myself — but I wondered.

In South Bend: "I'm worried about his health. If he

doesn't start eating soon, I'm going to make him see a doctor."

In Fort Wayne: "He'll be having his birthday when we're in Chicago. Let's go halves and get Sarah's ring out of hock. Gus said he'll wire the money to the pawn-shop and have them mail it to the Hotel Sherman."

In Indianapolis, the morning after we'd played a one-nighter at the Rainbow Room of the Barclay Hotel, Polly, Harry, and I went down to the coffee shop together. Augie and Buddy had just finished their breakfast.

"Our stuff's still set up in the Rainbow Room," Augie said as they were leaving. "Stop by when you've eaten. We've got something we want you to hear."

Instead of the milk toast he'd been surviving on, Harry ordered bacon and eggs and a stack of wheatcakes. He ate every speck and then signaled the waitress.

"You won't believe this," he said. "But I'm still hungry."

Polly smiled at him, rather tenderly, I thought, and for a moment I found myself wishing that Gus had never kicked that tire.

"Maybe you should order a carryout," I said to Harry. "To hold you till lunch."

In the Rainbow Room, the chairs were stacked on the tables. Two cleaning ladies were polishing the mirror that lined the wall behind the bar, and a janitor was vacuuming the carpet. Basil was folding our music stands, but the drums and string bass hadn't been packed.

"Hey, wait'll you hear what Augie and Buddy have worked out," Basil called when he saw us coming in. "Fiddlesticks."

"Fiddlesticks?" Harry said. "What the hell's that?"

Augie grinned. "Very simple," he said, picking up a pair of drum sticks. "Sticks on a fiddle."

"Play us a little number, Harry," Buddy said. "We'll show you."

Harry sat down at the piano and ran his fingers across the keys in a series of *arpeggios.* "What do you want?" he asked them. "Fast? Slow?"

"In between," Buddy said. "Do a few bars of 'Jersey Bounce.' "

"Jersey Bounce" was a smooth swing number. Harry did a little flourish in the upper register for an opening, and then went into the song's basic riff with his left hand. Buddy quickly picked up the rhythm, plucking the strings of his bass — in jazz, the string bass was always played *pizzicato* — in a four-four beat. Then, with his left hand still on the fingerboard of the instrument, fingering the melody, he removed his right hand from the strings, and Augie took over with his drum sticks, playing the strings with the same accents and rolls he would use on a snare drum. The rhythm was infectious, and we all started rocking with the music.

"Groovy!" Polly cried, clapping her hands. "Make it dance, Augie."

He did, and the effect was of a dancer tapping his shoes in melody. Harry wrapped it up with a sweeping *arpeggio,* followed by three crashing chords in the lower register. Polly and Basil and I gave them a big round of applause.

"Which strings were you playing off, Augie?" I asked him.

"The middle ones," he said. "The A and the D. With

a little practice, I should be able to hit a few accent shots on the side ones, the E and the G."

"It's really marvelous," Polly said. "You ought to get Gene to work that routine into some of our arrangements."

"He'd never buy it," Buddy said. "You know Gene — no improvisation."

"But it'll be swell for our combo," Basil said. "And I could sit in on drums while you're doing it. Maybe a little soft two-beat on the snare."

"That's right," Augie said. "We could do a lot of stuff like that in a combo."

"Speaking of our ombo-cay," Buddy said. "All five members are present and accounted for."

"All four members," Polly corrected him. "I still haven't said I'm in."

"Well, let's pretend you are," Buddy said, "and jam a little."

"Suits me," I said.

"I'll unpack your clarinet, Skeets," Basil said, and he hurried over to the equipment trunks that were lined up to one side of the bandstand.

"When do we have to catch the bus?" Harry said.

"No bus," Polly said. "We're taking a train to Chicago. We've got plenty of time."

It was the first time we'd ever played together, and I was a little nervous.

"How about 'Jersey Bounce'?" I suggested as I moistened the reed of my clarinet.

"Let's make it 'Blue Skies,'" Harry said. "Is E-flat okay with you, Buddy?"

74

"Yeah, E-flat's fine," Buddy said. "Skeets, why don't you figure out a little arrangement?"

"Who needs it?" Augie said. "We'll improvise. Ready? Uh-one and uh-two —"

Harry, who had a perfect sense of pitch, set our style in the first few bars, playing a deep, throbbing rhythm with his left hand and establishing the melody in sharp, quick *glissandos* with his right. I found myself coming in almost naturally, playing a smooth, mellow counterpoint to Harry, with Augie and Buddy backing us with the kind of pulsing rhythmic attack that made you want to give your best.

They were great musicians. Augie maintained a steady four-four beat on the bass drum, while playing his cymbal accents in two-four, with an occasional rim shot on the snare drum. Buddy had a fine sense of timing and pacing. When Harry signaled Polly to come in on vocal, he came down the scale two-beat and gave her a perfect introduction.

Polly's clear voice blended into our evolving style. I gave her a background of soft little figures on my clarinet. When she finished, I was playing directly to her, and she was singing to me.

"Solid!" Buddy called out.

Harry did one final chorus and then went into a *cadenza* like no *cadenza* I'd ever heard, restating the theme in the lower register, while playing a dozen variations on it with his right hand. I identified snatches of Bach, Respighi, and another composer I wasn't sure of. As Harry built to a climax, Augie came in with a crescendo on the snare drum. Then, with a crashing of cymbals and the piano holding the final chord in *tremolo* — we finished.

"Wow!" Augie said, out of breath and perspiring heavily. "That was wild."

"We're good," Buddy said, smiling with pleasure. "You know that? We're really good."

"I really enjoyed it," said Polly. "It's lots more fun than the band."

"It's the freedom of it," Harry said. "A combo lets your spirit soar."

In the band, we always gave our best; Gene would tolerate no less. But at times, we reached for more, for those electrical moments that all musicians have experienced but no musician can describe, moments when we soared into a mystical dimension of artistic expression. They came rarely, unexpectedly, but they were what we lived for. We had come close on "Blue Skies." Very close. The janitor unstacked the chairs from one of the tables, and we all sat down, full of ideas for the combo.

"Who was that last composer you quoted?" I asked Harry. "I caught Bach and Respighi — who was the last one?"

"Paganini," he replied. "It's from one of his *Caprices.*"

"You could work a lot of the classics into our arrangements," Buddy said.

"And unusual instruments," I said. "A recorder would blend well with some of Harry's solos."

"Can you play the recorder, Skeets?" Buddy asked.

"Sure," I said. "The recorder and the ocarina, even the piccolo."

"Artie Shaw's talking about forming a combo with

a harpsichord in it," Augie said. "Won't that be somethin'?"

"Augie," Harry said, "you're the last of the big spenders. First a vibraphone, now a harpsichord."

"Which brings up the matter of financing," Buddy said. "Skeets, have you done any good on those estimates?"

"A little," I said. "Ellen's getting me some figures. I should have it all together by Chicago. Let's have a business conference on our day off."

"Can't," Augie said. "I've got an aunt in Evanston. She's invited Buddy and me for the day."

"I'm going up to Waukesha," Basil said. "I haven't been home since last summer."

"But Skeets and I are having a birthday dinner for Harry," Polly protested. "At Henrici's. We thought you'd all be there."

"Henrici's?" Basil said. "I'll be there. It's only two hours from Waukesha."

He got to his feet and started to pack my clarinet.

"Well," he said. "It's nice that the combo is definitely a quintet."

"Is it, Polly?" Augie asked her. "Are you in?"

She gave a deep sigh. "I just can't say for sure, Augie," she said. "Skeets and Harry and I are going out to Saint Mary's when we're in Chicago. I'll make up my mind after I've talked to Sister Angela."

We helped Basil with the rest of his packing. As Buddy was wrapping flannel around the tuning pegs of his string bass, he suddenly looked over toward the entrance of the Rainbow Room.

"Did you see what I saw?" he said.

"What?" I said.

"I could've sworn it was Gus," he said. "It looked like he'd been standing behind that big potted fern and then took a powder out the door."

"What on earth would he do that for?" Polly said.

"Spying on us, I'll bet," Harry said. "He'll probably blab everything he heard to Gene."

"So what?" Augie said. "The combo's no secret."

"I know," Harry said. "But when Gus starts sneaking around like that, it means trouble."

But even Harry couldn't dampen our spirits that day. We knew that we had the potential of a good combo, a successful combo. As we boarded a train to Chicago, I felt confident that we could resolve the problem of financing, even if we had to eat beans and sleep in cars. After all, big oaks from little acorns grow.

A New Focus

Chicago! Chicago!

Coming in on the Illinois Central railroad, you saw the best and the worst of it — the slums, the stockyards, the grimy factory neighborhoods; then the Loop, the domed skyscrapers, the magnificent parks and fountains, and the drawbridges going up over the river. Chicago had a beat all its own, an exciting surging rhythm that never let up.

"We'll go out to Des Plaines on the commuter line," Polly said as our train raced along Lake Michigan. "We're invited for lunch, and then Sister Angela has arranged a little program in the afternoon. Gus phoned Henrici's for seven o'clock reservations. We'll be back in plenty of time."

"How much did it cost to get Harry's ring out of hock?" I asked her.

"Fifty dollars," she said. "Plus interest."

"Whew! That's a pretty rich birthday cake."

We were booked for two nights at the Panther Room, that pulsating, low-ceilinged room in the Hotel Sherman, where waiters in turbans and satin jodhpurs served beef tenderloin on flaming swords. Other clubs swung; the Panther Room thundered. And in our opening set, we caught fire and started reaching for it, nearly blowing the roof off. Gene quickly slammed on the brakes.

"What's he afraid of, anyway?" Harry complained afterward. "We were really soaring. Woody Herman and his Herd will be here after us. We could've left them something to shoot at."

"I don't see why it's so important, Harry," Polly said. "We're number two in *Down Beat.* Isn't that enough?"

"It's not just the polls, Polly. It's a matter of . . . of —" He snapped his fingers at me.

"A matter of artistic integrity," I said.

"Exactly."

Thursday was a day off, our last until Los Angeles. It was a beautiful spring day, cool and sunny, with puffs of white clouds in the sky. Everyone was in a good mood. Gus had finally heard from his son, Bert — a pile of letters all at once, as Ellen had predicted. Gene and Ellen were going to spend the day at the Field Museum and the Planetarium, and then have dinner with some of Ellen's friends in Winnetka. There was only one gloomy note: Bobby Consiglio, who played second trombone, received his induction notice for the army.

"When do you have to report?" Augie asked him.

"Two weeks after we get back to New York," Bobby said.

"Maybe you'll get an assignment in music," Buddy said. "An army band or something."

"Fat chance," Bobby said. "The army doesn't have enough marching bands for all the musicians they're gonna draft. I'm cooked. I'll end up in the infantry."

At the last minute, Harry had to cancel out of our trip to St. Mary's. His father was in town on business, and he and Harry were having lunch together.

"He said he's got something important to discuss," Harry said.

"Don't forget tonight," Polly reminded him. "We'll meet you in the lobby at six-thirty."

St. Mary's was twenty miles northwest of Chicago. We took a commuter train to Des Plaines, and then a bus out to the orphanage. It was Polly's first visit since she'd joined the band. The day before, she'd spent two hours at Marshall Field's choosing a new dress, but instead had on a two-piece polka-dot outfit she'd made herself at St. Mary's.

"The new one looks too expensive," she said. "The kids might think I was showing off."

As we transferred to the bus, she had a moment of panic. "Let's go back, Skeets," she said. "I'll come back after the tour."

I had to shove her up the steps of the bus, and then she slouched in her seat, biting her nails.

"Listen, Polly," I said. "You think you're different because of Saint Mary's, but you're not. I feel the same way when I go home."

"You're just saying that," she said gloomily.

"I mean it," I said. "Once when I was going home from Juilliard, I got as far as Norfolk and turned back."

"Because of the situation with your father?"

"Not entirely. I was just scared."

"But why, Skeets? A person should feel happy to be going home."

"I don't know," I said. "Maybe it's just the being away. A place like New York changes you, and you're not sure your family will approve."

"That's how I feel now," Polly said. "That they won't like me. That I haven't lived up to their expectations."

"Well, if it's any help," I said, "they're probably just as nervous as you are."

The bus was approaching a crossroads. Polly sat up straight and pointed out the landmarks of her childhood — the general store where Sister Angela had bought her Popsicles; the silo that she'd tried to climb when she was five years old; the creek where she'd gone wading. Then St. Mary's came into view, very much as Polly had described it: a large brick building, four stories, set far back from the road in a grove of maple trees. A white cross gleamed from the rooftop. The setting was lovely, but the building reminded me of the state mental hospital back in Virginia.

"Look, Skeets," she said. "My former pupils. I taught first grade my last year here."

Children were pouring from the main entrance, waving wildly.

"You taught school?" I said. "You never told me that."

"There are lots of things I haven't told you." The bus was coming to a stop. Polly grabbed my hand and pulled me impatiently to the front exit.

And then she was leaping off the bus and gathering up armloads of laughing children. Children appeared from every direction. And nuns, in their black Franciscan habits, with long strings of rosary beads clattering from their waists. One of them stood out from the others, with serene eyes and a quiet air of authority — a pale-skinned woman, slight in stature and much younger than I'd expected. Polly saw her coming and paused uncertainly. Then she burst into tears and ran into Sister Angela's outstretched arms.

"I've prayed every night for this moment," she said, clasping Polly tightly to her breast. "Welcome home, dear."

My memory of St. Mary's is a montage of images — long linoleumed corridors smelling faintly of disinfectant, eager children struggling for attention, Polly searching for mementos of her life and finding none.

"It's as if I've been erased," she remarked sadly. "When you leave here, everything gets handed down — your bed, your books, your clothes."

A military honor roll hung outside the chapel, with gold stars after the names of three of her classmates who had been killed in action. "The boys have been enlisting the minute they come of age," Sister Angela said. "And the girls have had no trouble finding jobs in the war plants. I'm afraid all of your old friends are gone, dear."

The noon meal had been held till our arrival. The food was simple but good — boiled beef, vegetables, a fruit cup, fresh-baked bread, and large pitchers of milk. Polly held court with her former pupils, while Sister Angela turned her attention to me. She talked about

St. Mary's, the football team she was organizing, the new courses in music appreciation.

"Pity you don't have a phonograph," I said. "It's hard to study the classical composers without records."

"Oh, but we do have a phonograph," she said. "Four of them, as a matter of fact; one for each floor, as well as an excellent record library. I'm surprised you didn't know. They were a gift from your employer."

"Gene?" I said, nearly choking on a mouthful of fruit.

"Of course," Sister Angela replied, and smiled. "Such a compassionate man."

After lunch, the institution's routine was resumed. Polly and I were left to ourselves until school let out. She took me on a tour of the building — the library, the gymnasium, the infirmary. In the third-floor dormitory, she showed me her old bed, more like a cot than a bed, next to a window that overlooked the maple grove. She sat down on the bed and ran her hands over the patched blanket.

"It's hard for me to believe that this was my home for seventeen years."

"You sound a little blue," I said.

"No, I'm all right." She sighed. "But it isn't how I thought it would be. So many of the kids are gone, and I'll probably never see them again. We shared so much, and now it's as if it didn't mean anything."

"It's like that at a regular school, Polly," I said. "There are buddies I know I'll never see again. I keep thinking I'll look them up, but I never do. Maybe certain friends are just for certain times."

Sister Angela had arranged a little talent show in the auditorium. We had a fine time, watching the children do their routines. When they finished, they begged Polly to sing a few songs, which she did — "Moon Love," "Skylark," and "A Stairway to the Stars." Then she gathered the children around her in a kind of chorus line.

"Remember the song about the roses we used to sing in class?" she asked them.

" 'Ring Around the Rosie'!" the children cried.

As they sang, Polly coached them in a little dance number, with the children kicking first one leg, then the other. The routine brought down the house.

"Sister Angela!" Polly called down to the audience. "Come join us!"

The sight of the nun kicking up her heels with Polly and the children brought a great round of applause.

"Lands!" she exclaimed, out of breath. "I've never seen Saint Mary's filled with such happiness!"

All too soon, it was time to leave.

"I'm glad I came, Polly," I said.

"I am too, Skeets," she said. "It's just as well that Harry didn't come. I would've felt embarrassed."

"Why? Harry isn't snooty."

"No," she said. "But his family has that big house in Poughkeepsie."

"So what?" I said. "My family has a nice house in Princess Anne."

"I know," she said. "But it's different with you."

When we left, Polly's little friends were lined up at the main entrance. She shook every hand, kissed every cheek. I walked on down to the road to flag the bus, while Polly and Sister Angela strolled in the maple grove. Watching them, it occurred to me that although Polly had no mother, she had a mother's love.

When the bus came, Polly clung to Sister Angela, but there were no tears. The tears came later, as the bus pulled away and the red brick building disappeared in the slanting late-afternoon sun. I pretended not to notice. It was a moment that couldn't be shared, but I knew what was going through her mind. St. Mary's was no longer a place to go home to. Polly had outgrown it. And the realization seemed to give new focus to her life.

That night, in the glow of candlelight at Henrici's, over fine food and sparkling Burgundy — Polly joined the combo.

"Whoopee!" Basil exclaimed.

"You won't regret it, Pols," Harry said.

"I'm not sure about that," she said. "Well — what's next? I haven't the faintest idea how you go about these things."

"The first thing, obviously, is money," Harry said. "Instruments for Augie and Buddy, transportation, uniforms for us and dresses for you — it all costs and what we need is a backer."

"Who backed Gene?" Polly asked.

"Are you kidding?" Harry said. "Gus."

"Gus?" Polly was incredulous. "I never knew that."

"Don't let those baggy pants fool you," Harry said. "He gets fifteen percent of everything." Harry told her about Gus and Gene's first meeting, in a musicians' hiring hall in Cleveland. Gene's first band had just folded, and he was flat broke. Gus owned a traveling carnival and was looking for someone to start a dance concession. But he was so impressed with Gene, he sold the carnival and staked him to a fresh start.

"No wonder they're always talking about the old days," Polly laughed. "Just think — every time Gus slaps a fine on Harry, he gets to keep part of it."

Our waiter asked if we were ready to order.

"Is it okay to order steak with mushrooms at Henrici's?" Basil asked Harry.

"Yes, Basil," Harry said. "You can order all the steak you want."

"Swell," Basil said, and to the waiter, "I'll have the porterhouse special — blood rare."

I had finally finished the cost estimates I'd promised. The hotel stenographer had typed them up and made copies, which I handed to Polly, Harry, and Basil.

"What's the tab come to, Skeeter?" Harry said.

"See for yourself," I said.

THE COMBO
Budget

(Figures are for a twelve-week period — four weeks of rehearsal, eight weeks on the road. A twenty percent fund is included for unforeseen expenses. Two totals: one with vibraphone, one without.)

String bass: $300.00

Trap drums: *One bass drum, one snare drum, two side tom-toms, one floor tom-tom, three crash cymbals, one high-hat cymbal, sticks, wire brushes, noisemakers, etc.*   600.00

Used car: *seven-passenger, Packard or La Salle.*   400.00

Car expenses: *gas, oil, etc.*   100.00

Music stands: *for clarinet, bass, and drums, $8.00 each; painted white with combo's name in dark blue.*   24.00

Salaries: *$300.00 a week. Augie, Buddy, Harry, Skeets, Polly: $55.00. Basil: $25.00.*	3,600.00
Road expenses: *Meals: $2.00 a day per person. Hotel: $2.50 a night per room. Three rooms: Polly; Skeets and Harry; Augie, Buddy, and Basil.*	1,092.00
Rehearsal studio: *four weeks; $25.00 a week.*	100.00
Publicity:	300.00
Miscellaneous: *clarinet reeds, music paper, instrument repair kits, catgut strings for bass fiddle, etc.*	20.00
Contingency fund:	1,287.00
TOTAL (without vibes)	$7,823.00
Vibraphone:	700.00
TOTAL (with vibes)	$8,523.00

"It's not as bad as I thought it'd be," Harry said.

"It's bad enough," I said, "when you don't have the money."

"What's a high-hat cymbal?" Polly asked.

"That's the one Augie plays with a pedal," Basil said. "It's got a nice tight sound."

"The budget's kind of cheap on the salaries," Harry remarked.

"Fifty-five bucks is what we started at in the band," I said. "We've got to sacrifice a little to get started. But we ought to work Basil up to forty a week as soon as we can."

"Forty bucks!" Basil said, smiling from ear to ear.

"How were things at home, Basil?" Polly asked him.

"Great," he said. "My mom's applied for a job at the motor works. They landed a bunch of war contracts and are hiring women for some of the jobs. I'll sure be glad to see her get out of that laundry."

Harry wondered about my entry for publicity.

"Ellen knows a young guy who's just starting out," I said. "She says he'll handle us for a hundred a month."

"It looks a lot simpler than I thought," Polly said. "We rehearse for a month, and then start making money."

Harry and I burst into laughter. "It's not that easy, Pols," Harry said. "Tell her the facts of life, Skeeter."

I poured myself another glass of wine and explained the economics of the music business to Polly.

"Bookings," I said. "Everything boils down to bookings. We may spend all our time on the road hustling for work or playing joints that don't pay beans." I told

her how Gene had done it, playing second-rate dates
until the band got booked into the Playland Casino in
Rye, New York. Gene had lost money on the deal, but
Playland had a radio wire — a half hour of network
time every night. After the radio exposure, he got
booked into all the big spots, the Palladium in Hollywood, the Panther Room, the Glen Island Casino out
on Long Island Sound, and went straight to the top.

"One big break is all we need," I said. "One good
booking that attracts national attention."

"But aren't there booking agencies?" Polly asked.

"The good ones won't look at you till you're estab-
lished," I said.

"Who handles Gene?"

"MAI," Harry said. "Musical Artists, Incorporated.
They're the best."

"Maybe I could work as an advance man," Basil
said. "You know, go on ahead to the next town and
drum up business."

"Not a bad idea," Harry said.

"It doesn't sound very encouraging," Polly said.

"Are you still in?" I asked her.

"Yes," she said emphatically. "We've got a good
combo. It's worth a few sacrifices."

We were almost through when Augie and Buddy
arrived.

"I thought you guys were out in Evanston," I said.

"We've just got a minute," Augie said. "My aunt
and uncle and cousin are waiting for us over at the
Oriental Theater. They wanted to see that new Spencer
Tracy flick."

"A boy cousin," Polly asked, "or a girl one?"

Buddy flashed his lewd grin. "A girl," he said. He cupped his hands over his chest and jiggled them. "What a set of knockers."

"Shame on you, Buddy," Polly said. "You've got a one-track mind."

They had brought a little birthday gift that made Harry roar with laughter. A string of fake pearls, with a note attached to it. *Observe the markings!*

"Hey, guys, this is swell," Harry said. "A genuine keepsake."

"We've gotta scram," Augie said. "Did you finish those estimates, Skeets?"

"Yes," I said, and pulled out copies of the budget, which they took with them.

"Now let's put the combo aside for a while," Polly said, signaling our waiter, "and get down to the purpose of this dinner."

It wasn't until the waiter brought out Harry's birthday cake that I realized that I'd drunk nearly a bottle of wine and was getting slightly looped. Polly had had only a few sips, and Harry, who'd drunk very little since Jiffy's, had had none at all.

"I chipped in on the cake, Harry," Basil said. "A third of it is my gift to you."

"Make a wish, Harry," Polly said.

It was a chocolate layer cake with white icing and twenty candles. Harry blew them out in one breath, and then Polly got his present from under the table. She had wrapped the ring in a hatbox stuffed with tissue paper. Harry held the box to his ear and listened suspiciously.

"It doesn't tick." He gave it a little shake. "And it doesn't rattle. I know. It's cash. Tens and twenties. Guys, you shouldn't have. And on your salaries."

Polly laughed till there were tears in her eyes.

When he rummaged through the tissue paper and found the ring, Harry was speechless. "Holy cow, if that isn't something! Polly, Skeeter — thanks. But you shouldn't have. Fifty bucks is a lot of dough."

"Don't be silly, Harry," Polly said. "You would've been out both the ring and the money. At least now you can return it and get back your down payment."

"Oh, I don't know." Harry held the ring up to the candle. "It's a nice ring. Maybe I'll hang on to it. Who knows? Sarah may get down off her high horse."

"Or you may want to marry some other girl," Basil said, "and you'll be all set. If she's got the same size finger, that is."

"This calls f'r a toast," I said.

"With what?" Polly said. "You drank all the wine."

"I'll order s'more."

"Don't you dare, Skeets. Your eyes are about to roll out of their sockets. We'll use our water glasses."

We raised our glasses, and Polly gave the toast. "To Harry, our favorite wise guy. With much love and many happy returns of the day." Then she leaned over and kissed him on the cheek.

"Don't stop, Pols," Harry teased her. "I'm supposed to get twenty."

"Not from me, you aren't," she said. "Now behave yourself and tell us about your father. You haven't said a word. Did you have a nice visit?"

"Well, yes and no —" Harry hesitated. "You're not

going to believe this, but he's taking a commission in the army."

"But why?" Polly said. "He's too old for combat, isn't he?"

"It's nothing like that, Pols. He's got a background in constitutional law, and they want him to work on military government. He says the United States will probably occupy a bunch of countries after the war."

Harry shook his head sheepishly.

"He wanted to know if I approved. Can you beat that? It should've been the other way around."

The waiter interrupted with our check. I reached for my wallet, but kept missing the pocket. My head was swimming from all the wine, and I was depressed over the way Polly had kissed Harry. I knew I was being unreasonable. The three of us were friends, that's all. So she had kissed Harry — so what? She'd kissed me often enough, hadn't she? Those quick, friendly kisses were almost a part of her nature. And she'd held my hand, and snuggled up to me on the bus without giving it a thought. But at St. Mary's, I had felt very close to her, and now it all seemed to be evaporating.

"Do you have enough money, Skeets?" she whispered as I fumbled with my wallet.

"Plenny," I said. My stomach was churning, and I was having difficulty telling a five from a ten. "Ah'm flush."

"Let me know my share," she said. "I'll get the money from Gus."

And then Harry, unwittingly, delivered the final blow. He and Polly had a series of dance numbers they did

with the band, short routines that Gene sometimes
worked in with Polly's vocals. As we stood up to leave,
Harry swept her into his arms, twirled her about, and
danced her to the door in a gliding fox-trot. It took only
a moment, but every eye in the crowded restaurant was
on them, and there was a ripple of applause. They
looked as though they belonged together, and I had a
premonition that Harry's ring would end up not on
Sarah's finger, but on Polly's —

"Oh, my gosh, he's white as a sheet!" Polly was
hurrying toward me, and then I felt myself being helped
to the door. "Quick, Basil, take his other arm!"

I came to in my bed at the hotel, in my underwear
and with a blanket thrown over me. Harry was snoring
in the other bed. My head throbbed, and there was a
bad taste in my mouth. Slowly, I propped myself up on
an elbow and turned on the reading lamp. My music
folder was on the nightstand. In my confused dreams,
an idea had come to me, and I didn't want it to slip
away. I took my World's Fair pen and printed on the
cover page of my symphonic suite:

"Pollyanna"
A TONE POEM FOR FLUTE AND ORCHESTRA
By Schuyler Sinclair

Then I reeled dizzily into the bathroom and was sick.

·8·
A Silent Presence

The road could be melancholy at times. When you
dedicate yourself to a career in music, you shut yourself
off from ordinary things, and there is much that you
miss.

That was the melancholy of the road. It hit us in
train stations at Christmas or Easter as we watched the
college kids heading home on vacation. It hit us even
worse at the college dances. It affected all of us, espe-
cially Polly and Basil, who watched the gaiety with
wistful eyes, like children who have been told they may
look but not touch.

Deep down, we knew those campus scenes weren't
always what they seemed to be. We had seen another
side — the boys retching on cheap whiskey, the girls
hurrying in from the parking lot, brokenhearted and
with their dresses torn. Still, it bothered us, and so when
we played the senior prom at the University of Illinois
in Champaign, we were glad we'd be leaving right after
the dance, on a 1 :00 A.M. train to Little Rock, Arkansas.
However, Champaign turned out to be different. Champaign was where we met Sally Sengstock.

Sally was the kind of girl you expected to meet at a midwestern university, but seldom did. Natural, unaffected, with a wholesome kind of beauty. She was chairman of the prom committee and was waiting to greet us when our bus pulled up at the student union.

"Lovely," Augie said when he saw her.

"A real dish," Buddy said. "Do you think she does one-nighters?"

Sally approached Gene very straightforwardly and extended her hand.

"We've planned some activities for you," she told him. "I hope you won't mind."

Gene did mind; he didn't like outsiders tampering with our schedule.

"We have a radio broadcast at six o'clock," he said. "We've got to rehearse." But when he learned that the activities included a chance for him to lecture at the music school, he became very cooperative.

Harry went into a spasm of suppressed laughter. "Now we know what makes Old Stone Face tick," he whispered to me. "He's a frustrated professor."

Harry may have been right. The students who jammed into a recital hall to hear him were dazzled by Gene's erudition. In twenty minutes, he surveyed the full spectrum of popular music, placing it in a historical perspective that ranged back to the Middle Ages. Then, to Gus's surprise and ours, he called on Gus, who kept the students in stitches with anecdotes about the logistics of a traveling dance orchestra — missed trains, lost instruments, vanished laundry. Afterward, at a reception in the student union, we had a pleasant chat with Sally

Sengstock, and I found myself wishing that we didn't have to catch that train.

"All that traveling must be exhausting," she said to Harry, who had scarcely taken his eyes off her since we stepped off the bus. "Do you have many engagements left?"

Harry did a little dance step and started to turn on the charm. Then, as though sensing that this girl was different, he straightened up and talked about the remainder of our schedule — the swing through the Southwest, the benefit performance in Council Bluffs, Iowa, after which we would head for the West Coast.

"We'll play a few dates in the Middle West on our way back," he said, "and then finish up in New York on June nineteenth."

"The nineteenth?" Sally said. "I'll have to tell my father. He'll be attending a dealers' convention in New York that week. He owns a hardware store in Galesburg."

At the mention of Galesburg, Harry and I exchanged amused glances. Sally gave us a quizzical look.

"Did I say something funny?" she said.

"Galesburg is sort of a joke with us," Harry explained. "We got snowbound in the depot there last winter. It was morning before they shoveled us out and took us up to the hotel for coffee."

"Why, of course!" Sally exclaimed, smiling brightly. "Then you've met my father. He was one of the men who shoveled you out. You couldn't have missed him. He wears a red mackinaw that stands out in the snow."

"Gee —" Harry said. "I really don't recall."

"I do," I said. "He had on one of those fur hats that state troopers wear."

"That was him," Sally said. She turned to Harry. "Do you believe in fate?"

"Not really," Harry said.

"Neither do I," she said. "But it makes you wonder, doesn't it? Here we've only just met, and already we have something in common."

When it was time for rehearsal, Sally insisted on escorting us to the gymnasium. "The campus can be confusing," she said. "Besides, I have to check on the decorations."

We strolled across a wide quadrangle shaded by tall elm trees. The bell in the clock tower tolled the quarter hour. We had noticed a tiny military ribbon pinned to Sally's blouse. Now Harry asked her about it. "It's the Navy Cross ribbon, isn't it?" he said.

"Yes," she said. "My brother's. He was killed in the Pacific last month." Suddenly her eyes filled with tears. She turned away from us. "I'm sorry," she said. "I haven't accepted it yet. We were very close. He was a senior when I was a freshman."

Harry put a hand on her shoulder. "Hey, you don't have to apologize," he said. "I guess we all know how rough it can be."

"No, you don't," Sally said. "Nobody does." Then she brushed a tear from her cheek and smiled. "But it's nice of you to say so."

We were in Champaign for eleven hours. Harry spent almost the whole time with Sally. She sat in on our rehearsal, stayed for our early radio broadcast,

and at the prom that night, she and her date ("Just a
friend," she assured Harry) were never far from the
bandstand.

"I wish he wouldn't rush her like that," Polly said.
"She's a nice girl, and he'll forget her the minute he
boards the train."

I hoped she was wrong. Harry was in a curious, re-
flective mood. Perhaps it was the prom. On the surface,
it was like any other prom — the corsages, the dance
cards, the garlands of flowers. But the war was a
silent presence in the air that night. Most of the boys
would be in uniform soon; many had already received
their orders. Tomorrow there would be tearful fare-
wells, but for now there was laughter and romance and
sweet music floating on perfumed air.

> *Cool it in the summer breeze,*
> *Serve it in the starlight underneath the trees,*
> *You'll discover tricks like these are sure to make*
> *your Moonlight Cocktail please.*

The dancers kept us on the stand for an extra set,
then crowded around the bandstand and gave us a big
round of applause. Buddy gazed at the array of pretty
girls. "All those lovelies," I heard him say. "I hope
they don't go to waste."

In our rush to make the train, no one noticed that
Harry had wandered off. "Honestly," Polly said. "If
he's up to his old tricks again —"

"Maybe he's with Gus and Ellen," I said. "They
went on ahead to confirm our reservations."

But when our bus arrived at the depot, we forgot all about Harry. Ellen was waiting in the parking lot, a tense look in her eyes.

"It's Gus —" she said. "Bert has been killed. He was in Doolittle's raid on Tokyo."

"Oh, how awful!" Polly said, and sagged against me.

"But I don't understand," I said. "Doolittle bombed Tokyo weeks ago."

"Bert's plane crashed in China after the raid. It wasn't confirmed until today."

What a rotten way to get the news, I thought, stranded in Illinois in the middle of the night.

"How is he going to get home at this hour?" I asked Ellen.

"Our train connects with an eastbound local in Effingham," she said. "I'll try to fill in for him while he's gone."

"Where is he, Ellen?" Polly asked.

"Inside. I told him to forget about the rest of the tour, but he insists on coming back. He'll try to catch up to us in Dallas or Houston."

Gus was slumped on a bench in the waiting room. Basil was next to him. Polly put her arms around Gus.

"Are you all right?" she said softly.

"Yeah, kitten. I'm okay."

"I don't know what to say, Gus." She buried her face against his chest and started crying.

"What's there to say?" Gus patted her shoulder. "It's the breaks, that's all."

"But it's cruel. You were so happy when you got those letters in Chicago."

"Mix-ups like that happen, kitten. There's a war on."

"Will there be a funeral or anything, Gus?" I asked.

"Maybe a memorial service, Skeets. The man from the War Department said they're sending a flag." He shook his head sadly. "I guess it'll be easier that way."

Looking into his tired eyes, I knew that nothing in the world was going to make it easier. We seldom thought of Gus as having a life apart from the band. He was always there, chartering buses, booking reservations, making sure we were fed and that our uniforms were cleaned and pressed. He'd worked hard for what he had, and now just when he should be enjoying it, his son was dead.

The other members of the band were filing into the waiting room to pay their respects — in little delegations, first Augie and Buddy, then the Mellow Birds, then the brass and reeds. "Sorry, Gus," they mumbled, or, "Tough luck, Gus," and Gus replied, "Thanks, kid."

Polly and I went outside. The platform was filling up with students who had come to see us off. A train whistle wailed in the distance.

"There's Harry," Polly said, and started for the parking lot. "I'd better break the news before he smarts off to Gus."

Harry, holding Sally Sengstock's hand, was climbing out of the rumble seat of a '36 Ford coupe. I looked for Sally's date, but didn't see him.

"I wonder how he arranged that," I said.

The train rumbled into the station in a shower of steam and sparks. We boarded at the observation car. Couples from the prom were still arriving, the girls in formal gowns, the boys in crisp white jackets. They lined the platform as we pulled out. "Good-bye!" they called to us. "Good luck!"

We waved from the observation platform.

"See you after the war!" Augie called back.

But would we? The train began to pick up speed. I looked back down the tracks, fixing the scene in my mind — the depot, the town, the towers of the university gleaming in the moonlight. I felt very proud that for a few hours I had been a part of it.

·9·
One of the Boys

There was a point in every road tour at which our perceptions blurred and we lost all sense of time or place. It was as if we were drifting on a stardust melody, to another club, another ballroom, briefly touching the lives of the dancers, then vanishing into the night.

After six shows and a war bond rally in Oklahoma City, Polly was asleep on her feet and couldn't remember where we were.

"Oklahoma City," I reminded her, amused. "We play Dallas tomorrow. Remember?"

"Are you sure?" she said vaguely. "I thought Dallas was yesterday."

It was a difficult week for me. When Harry mailed a card to Sally Sengstock, I began to hope that something serious was developing between them. But by the end of the week, Champaign appeared to be a forgotten interlude, and he picked up with Polly where he left off. Or did she pick up with him? The situation, if there was a situation, confused me. In Dallas, they hurried off to an all-night Chinese place. They invited me to go along, but I sensed I'd be in the way. And in Houston, when

a weathered rancher cornered Polly and drunkenly pro-
posed marriage, she grabbed Harry and introduced
him as her husband. It was a fine ploy, but it bothered
me; I wished she'd grabbed me instead.

Gus rejoined the band in Dallas. There had been a
few small comforts for him and Sadie. Bert had been
awarded the Distinguished Flying Cross, posthumously,
and Colonel Jimmy Doolittle had sent a letter of sympathy, which Gus planned to frame.

"He said Bert was the best pilot in the squadron,"
he said with pride.

We were glad he was back. Ellen had done her best,
but we had come to appreciate how indispensable Gus's
firm ways were to the band. We all did what we could
to make things easier for him, even Harry, who was
more punctual, less argumentative. There was one bad
moment, however. Between shows in Fort Worth, we
went over to a nearby park for a game of softball. Gene
hit a home run his first time at bat. Harry watched from
the sideline as he rounded the bases.

"Look at him huff and puff," he said, laughing. "He'll
never make it in the army."

"Tell us all about it, Mr. Draft Dodger," Gus said.

"Don't knock it, Gus," Harry said lightly. "Better
a live draft dodger than a dead —"

He caught himself too late. Gus's eyes blazed.

Polly tried to patch things up. "He didn't mean it,
Gus," she said.

"I know he didn't, kitten," Gus replied. "I just wish
the kid would wise up."

Polly was upset; dissension in the band always upset

her. She was playing right field, and in the next inning, she stumbled and fell going after a fly ball. For a moment, she didn't get up. I raced over to help her.

"I'm okay, Skeets." She was having trouble catching her breath. "It just knocked the wind out of me."

"You're sure it's not one of your spells?"

"Yes, I'm sure."

But I wasn't, and on the bus that night, I couldn't sleep, keeping an eye on her to make sure she was all right. As I sat alone with my thoughts, I began to see how hard it was for her to plan her life. No parents, no warm family memories, only Sister Angela and the friends she'd made in the band. The combo had given her a direction, but was it the right one? Her heart spells came on her unexpectedly, she'd told me. Perhaps the job Sister Angela had offered her would be better. But St. Mary's would surely take her out of my life, and the thought depressed me.

I brooded long into the night. We were heading back north, to Iowa for a Navy Relief benefit. As we neared the Oklahoma line, Basil came back from the front of the bus.

"Are you awake, Skeets?" he whispered.

"Unfortunately," I said. "Sometimes you get so tired you can't sleep."

"I wish these buses had toilets," he said.

"It's a long haul between gas stations in Texas," I said. "Can you hold out till Durant? We'll ask the driver to stop."

"I guess so," Basil said. "You feel like talking?"

"Sure, Basil," I said. "Let me get Polly tucked in."

I arranged Polly so that she was curled up across both seats and bundled her up warmly. We took seats across the aisle. "What chance do we have of coming up with money for the combo?" Basil asked me.

I laughed. "Like a snowball in hell, probably."

"I'm serious, Skeets."

"I don't know, Basil," I said. "I've thought about trying to borrow the money from my father, but he'd laugh me out of the house."

"What about Harry? His dad's pretty well-heeled."

"That's a possibility," I said. "But his father will be losing a lot of income when he goes into the army. Why all the questions, Basil?"

"There's a problem at home."

"But I thought things were looking up."

"That's the problem. They are. Now that my mom got that job at the motor works, she wants me to come home and go back to school."

"It's a good idea, Basil," I said. "A diploma's important, and Waukesha High is a fine school."

We had visited Waukesha with Basil one afternoon when the band played a date at the Schroeder Hotel in Milwaukee. We met Basil's mother, a small vigorous woman, and his two sisters, Patsy, eight, and Mary June, who was ten. We had visited the high school, where Mr. Worthington, the principal, expressed great interest in Basil's work with the band.

"It's just a routine job," Harry had told him, "but Basil has made it something more."

We had ended up at the Sugar Bowl, where the after-school crowd hung out. Basil was the center of attention.

"Augie Renna's teaching me to play the drums," he told the excited kids. And he gave them a demonstration, using a pair of knives for sticks and the marble top of the soda fountain for a drum. It had been a pleasant afternoon, and I thought Basil had best forget the combo and go home and be a kid again.

"But the combo's a swell opportunity, Skeets," he said. "I'm going to be a good drummer one day, and it'll give me some great experience."

"Then it's the combo," I said. "Right?"

"Right," Basil said. "Gee, thanks, Skeets. You've been a big help."

The road was full of surprises. Just when you thought you couldn't stand another cramped bus, another day without a shower, something would happen to renew your spirits.

Late that afternoon, shortly after we had crossed into Iowa, the bus suddenly slowed and turned down a narrow farm road that wound through freshly plowed fields.

"We're going to Mineola," Basil reported. "The farm where Gene grew up. He wants to show Ellen the place."

The bus pulled up in front of a large farmhouse, white with green shutters, shaded by two enormous oak trees. No one appeared to be living in it; there was a FOR SALE sign on the lawn, and the windows were bare of curtains.

"We'll just be a few minutes," Gene said to us as he and Ellen got off the bus.

We watched with smiles as they strolled hand in

hand up the long, curving driveway. Gene pointed up
to a dormer window on the second floor — his old bed-
room, I supposed. There was an old tire suspended
from a limb of one of the oak trees. "I'll bet he swings
her," Polly said, giggling. Ellen appeared to protest at
first; then she kicked off her shoes, sat down in the tire,
and Gene began to swing her.

They were still holding hands when they got back on
the bus and we started for Council Bluffs.

"I haven't had so much fun since I was a schoolgirl,"
Ellen said, smiling radiantly.

Council Bluffs was another surprise. Our date was
at a country club above the Missouri River. Since it was
a benefit, we were extended full privileges of the club.
Gus even waived the rules on drinking; we would be
leaving for Seattle in the morning, and there would be
time to recuperate on the train. "But anyone who's late
for the bus," he warned us, "will spend the rest of the
tour working off the fine."

After the last set, we all converged on the bar. Some
of the sidemen brought their instruments in from the
bandstand. Soon a fine jam session was in progress, with
Harry on piano and Basil filling in for Augie on drums.
I sat in for a few licks on clarinet, then dropped out to
join Polly, who was sharing a booth with Gene and
Ellen.

Gene was in an expansive mood. He ordered bour-
bon and water and talked about baseball, the war, and
the new trends in popular music. Polly took advantage
of his good spirits to ask about his plans for after the
war.

"Who knows?" he replied. "Things are so unsettled."

"But you'll form another band, won't you?"

"I don't know, Polly. A successful orchestra is a special combination of talents. I doubt if I could put it together again."

He paused to listen to the jam session. They were doing "One O'Clock Jump," with an intricate drum solo — only wire brushes on the snare drum and an occasional accent on the high-hat cymbal.

"Basil's really good," Gene said. "Good enough for your combo, Skeets."

I grinned. "So you've heard about it."

"I hear about everything. I may work that fiddlesticks routine into one of our numbers before the tour's over."

"What do you think our chances are?" Polly asked him.

"Excellent," he said. "Would you headline the group?"

"We haven't even talked about that yet," Polly said.

"It wouldn't be a bad idea," Gene said. "With the right arrangements and a good combo backing you, you could be a smash. It won't be easy, but you can do it."

"Would it be harder than the band?" Polly asked.

"Much harder. But you'll have a big advantage over the competition,"

"What's that?" I said.

"Me."

"Seriously?" Polly said.

"Of course. Have you forgotten? I'm still your guardian."

"No, Gene," Polly said, blushing. "I haven't forgotten."

"Half the battle is a good booking agency," he said. "When you get it all together, I'll put in a word for you at MAI."

"That's swell, Gene," I said. "But unless we come up with some financing, there'll be nothing to pull together."

Gene took a long sip from his drink. "Well, I'll tell you, Skeets," he said. "My experience has been that if you've got the talent and determination, money has a way of taking care of itself."

Normally, Gene was a sparing drinker — an occasional highball, sometimes two. That night, I lost track at six. I had never seen him so relaxed. When Basil urged him to join the jam session, he blew a loud Dixieland *glissando* and led the group into a jumping rendition of "Limehouse Blues."

"It's going to be a long night," Ellen said, smiling.

The bar was crowded and noisy, and the smoke was hurting Polly's eyes. "Let's get some fresh air, Skeets," she suggested. "And then I'd better turn in."

The clubhouse opened on a terraced lawn that overlooked the wide Missouri. It was a clear night with a crescent moon. Polly kicked off her shoes and skipped in the damp grass.

"I'm glad Gene was so talkative," she said. "I feel much more confident about the combo."

"Is your health up to it?" I asked her. "You heard what he said about how hard it would be."

"It won't be that hard. I can pace myself."

"Why don't you find out for sure?" I suggested. "See a doctor when we get back to New York, and find out exactly what you're capable of."

"All right," she agreed.

"Another thing," I said. "I think your heart problem should be out in the open. Everyone in the combo should help make things easier for you."

"That's very thoughtful of you, Skeets," she said softly.

"I'm just being practical."

Sounds of gaiety drifted out from the bar. The jam session had progressed into a sing-along.

"I'd better call it a night," Polly said. "Are you going back to the bar?"

"For a while," I said. "Sounds like quite a party."

"Should I stop by your room in the morning?"

"You'd better," I said. "You'll probably have to pry Harry and me out of bed."

But Harry and I made the bus with time to spare. To everyone's amazement, it was Gene who was late. Harry was beside himself with glee.

"This I've got to see," he said.

It was one of the major events of the tour. Old Stone Face had broken a rule. Gus glanced impatiently at his watch; the rest of us milled around the bus. Finally, Gene straggled out of the clubhouse — unkempt, unshaven, and with no necktie. We stood aside as he approached Gus.

" 'Morning, Gus," he said, and fumbled for a cigarette.

" 'Morning, Gene," Gus said, giving him a hard look. "Oversleep?"

"Something like that." Gene squirmed in embarrassment. "Well, what are we waiting for?"

"In a minute, Gene." Gus made some notations on his clipboard. "Let's see now. Late for the bus, five bucks. No shave, two bucks. No tie, another two bucks. No shine, a buck. Near as I can figure, that's an even ten bucks."

Gene stared at him haplessly.

"Cash?" he said. "Or will you take a check?"

Gus struggled to keep a straight face. Then someone giggled, and the whole band broke into laughter.

"Okay, okay!" Gus barked. "Let's get the show on the road!"

We clambered aboard the bus. The toughest part of the tour lay ahead, we knew, but our morale was soaring.

Old Stone Face had become one of the boys.

·10·
A Silver Wand

Seattle was blue skies and sailboats gleaming in Puget Sound. Portland was sunshine and roses and Mt. Hood floating on the eastern horizon. But San Francisco was drizzle and fog — and a doctor rushing backstage after Polly collapsed in the middle of our last show at the Orpheum Theater. Remarkably, when the excitement was over, her heart condition remained a secret shared only by me.

"Didn't he use a stethoscope?" I asked her afterward.

"No. He just took my temperature and felt my pulse. But I sort of led him off the track."

"How?"

"I told him I had the curse." She blushed.

"The what?" I said.

"You know, that time of the month."

"Oh." Now I blushed, too.

"And what did you tell Gus?"

"That it was the veal cutlets at that greasy spoon in Portland."

"Aw, Polly, that's not fair. Gus ought to know."

"You're not going to tell him, are you?"

"I should."

"You promised not to. Remember?"

"I know, but this is different."

"What's different about it? A promise is a promise."

I was concerned that she was exceeding her endurance and might permanently damage her health. But I couldn't help admiring her determination to stick with the tour to the end.

"Well, try to take it easy, will you?" I said. "Holy cow, you could've fallen off the stage."

As it was, the audience had had no idea what was happening. We had been doing "My Blue Heaven." The spotlight had just moved from Polly and the Mellow Birds to Harry, who had an eight-bar solo. The rest of the stage was in shadow. I heard a slight commotion and glanced up. The Mellow Birds had formed a circle around Polly and were moving her offstage. Mike Chapman had his arm around her waist and was rocking slowly with the music, so as not to attract attention. Polly's face was white, and her arms hung down limply. Gus was out from the wings in a flash, signaling to Gene, who quickly called a cut. We went straight into the next number, a boogie-woogie instrumental, and no one was the wiser.

The doctor had already left by the time the curtain closed and the movie began. It was nearly midnight. A bus was waiting in the alley to take us to Fresno.

"Everybody relax," Gus said, keeping his voice low. "She's okay. Just a little stomach upset."

Polly, pale but smiling, had changed into a shirtwaist

dress. She was stretched out on a stack of quilted scenery pads. Gene and Ellen were with her. Gene shook his head doubtfully.

"Maybe we should put her on a train to New York," he said to Ellen. "I think she needs a good rest."

I felt my heart sink. If Polly was sent back, she would go out of my life forever. I couldn't imagine her not sitting next to me on the bus or giving me her jelly at breakfast. We were all showing signs of strain. Gene looked tired and drawn, Ellen had been complaining of headaches, and now Polly had collapsed. Bands had fallen apart on the road before, I knew, even some of the big ones. I held my breath, waiting for Gene's decision.

"We've got a day off coming up in Los Angeles," Ellen was saying to him. "She can lie on the beach and get plenty of rest."

"But look at her," Gene said. "She can hardly stay awake."

Polly was stifling a yawn.

"Oh, don't be silly, Gene," she said. "The doctor gave me a sedative."

Gus had been standing quietly in the shadows. Now he moved forward and made Gene's decision for him.

"We started together," he said. "We'll finish together."

He turned to Basil.

"Run out and make sure they've got plenty of blankets and pillows on that bus."

Then he lifted Polly into his arms and started for the door. The rest of us watched in silence as the two of them moved through the flickering light of the movie screen, Gus in his baggy pants and Polly cradled in his arms.

"Well, what are you guys waiting for?" he said, looking back at us. "Hustle your bustles!"

Over the next few days, it seemed we played every military base in California. Gene wanted to limit Polly to two numbers a show, but she was so obviously full of vitality, he relented.

"The army camps are fun," she told him. "It's the stage shows that are hard. Everything's so rigid."

Ironically, her remark also applied to the kind of dates our combo would play, but I didn't say anything. We had all been too tired to do much thinking about the combo, although I had talked to Harry about the possibility of his father's backing us.

"I've thought of it, too," he said. "I think there's a good chance he would."

"As an investment?" I asked him.

"No, I think he'd do it as a straight loan," he said. "I'll ask him after he gets settled in the army."

It was our first genuine ray of hope. "Maybe Gene was right," I said to Polly. "If you're really determined, maybe money will take care of itself."

But all the determination in the world wasn't going to alter the grim fact of the war. In Sacramento, at the Tremont Hotel, our mail caught up to us. Ellen passed it out in the coffee shop as we were having breakfast, Harry and I, Augie and Buddy. There was a letter for Augie in an official-looking envelope. He opened it gingerly.

"Rats," he said, shaking his head sadly. "Ain't that a kick in the keister?"

It was his induction notice. He read the opening paragraph aloud.

GREETINGS:

HAVING SUBMITTED YOURSELF TO A LOCAL BOARD COMPOSED OF YOUR NEIGHBORS FOR THE PURPOSE OF DETERMINING YOUR AVAILABILITY FOR TRAINING AND SERVICE IN THE LAND OR NAVAL FORCES OF THE UNITED STATES, YOU ARE HEREBY NOTIFIED THAT YOU HAVE BEEN SELECTED FOR TRAINING AND SERVICE THEREIN.

"Very impressive," Buddy said, reading the entire notice. "I wonder if I'm gonna get one of these greetings."

"I'm glad I don't have to worry about it," Harry said.

"You lucky stiff," Augie said. He pushed his bacon and eggs away. "I guess the army cuts your hair pretty short," he said, smiling nervously and running his fingers through his thick black hair.

"Short?" Buddy said. "You'll be scalped. And then they sprinkle it with some kind of chemical to make sure you don't have lice."

"Well, that's it for our combo," I said, and started to get up. "Without a drummer, we're dead, and I don't know who'd take a gamble on a dream. I'd better break the news to Polly and Basil."

"Wait a minute, Skeets," Augie said. "Aren't you forgetting something?"

"What?"

"Basil."

"Hey, that's right," I said. "Do you think he could handle it?"

"He's good and getting better. I could really work hard with him after we get back to New York."

"When do you have to report?"

"Sixty days. I'll have time to work with Basil and still make a trip home."

"What'll you use for drums?" Harry asked him. "After we break up, you'll be a drum-less drummer."

"Maybe your old man will come up with the financing by then," Augie said. "If not, I'll rent some drums."

It was a possibility — barely. But Basil, too, had received a letter that day. He told me about it on the bus to Santa Barbara.

"It was from my mother," he said. "Remember Mr. Worthington, the principal of Waukesha High?"

"A nice man," I said. "Harry and I talked with him while you were looking up your old geometry teacher."

"I guess he was pretty impressed by that conversation," Basil said. "He'll allow me a few credits for my work with the band and then give me a test to see how well I've kept up with my studies. If I do okay, he'll let me graduate with my class."

"You'd be foolish to turn down an offer like that," I said.

"I'm not going to," he said. "But a diploma isn't the main reason. My mom told me that one of my best buddies got killed in the war. He was a year ahead of me and joined the merchant marine as soon as he graduated. His ship was torpedoed in the North Atlantic."

"And so you feel the war sneaking up on you," I said.

"It's getting pretty close. Raymond Gram Swing says it might last five years. Augie and I are apt to end up sharing a foxhole."

"I understand, Basil," I said. "Go home to your family while you still can."

"It's been wonderful, the way you and Augie and all the others have treated me," he said. "I never dreamed I'd be turning down a chance to play drums in a big-time combo."

"Well, the war won't last forever, Basil," I said. "Maybe there's still hope."

"And will I still be on your list?"

"At the top of it."

"Gee, thanks, Skeets," he said. "You're a swell guy."

"The feeling's mutual, Basil."

And so the dream was over. Polly accepted the situation surprisingly well. "It was a good dream," she said with a sigh. "Do you realize we started talking about it the first day of the tour? I'd grown very fond of our nonexistent combo."

I felt devastated. I'd pinned all my hopes of staying close to Polly on the combo and now I'd run out of possibilities. I felt resentful toward the war.

The tour was beginning to wind down. Two nights at the Palladium Ballroom in Hollywood, a few dates back in the Middle West — St. Louis, Louisville, and Peoria, Illinois — and it would be over. On the bus to Los Angeles, Harry was full of plans for a night on the town.

"Gus says we'll be at the hotel by eight," he said. "Let's go dancing."

"Where?" Polly asked.

"Ciro's," he said. "If we can get reservations. Okay with you, Skeeter?"

"I don't think so, Harry," I said. "I'm bushed."

But I really wasn't that tired. In my dark mood, Harry had become a target of my resentment — his phony draft deferment, the easy way he'd charmed Polly. I turned petulantly to the window. We were coming down the Coast Highway, north of Malibu, past rocky shoals and sheltered coves where the surf broke in sprays of white. A flight of navy planes swooped low over a stretch of sandy beach.

"The ocean's so peaceful," Polly said. "It's hard to believe there's a war going on out there."

We watched the planes disappear on the horizon. The sun was setting, making iridescent motes in Polly's hair. Harry had moved to the front of the bus, chatting with Augie and Buddy. "I wish Harry would find himself a new playmate," Polly said, frowning. "I'm tired of being a substitute for Sarah. Pretty soon he'll make a pass at me, and then what'll I do?"

I looked at her in confusion. Had I been wrong about her feelings for Harry? Was he, after all, merely one of her wounded birds?

"I wish you'd change your mind, Skeets," she said, "and come with us tonight."

"Okay," I agreed quickly.

"Seriously?"

"Yes, but no dancing."

She smiled. "Not even if I wear flat shoes?"

"Well, in that case —"

The road curved away from the ocean. We came up over the Santa Monica Mountains, and then Los Angeles was below us. Even with the dimout, it stretched like a jeweled carpet in the California dusk. Polly pressed close to the window.

"It's always a thrill, isn't it?" she said. "Let's forget all the might-have-beens. Let's go everywhere and do everything."

Southern California held a special magic for us. Perhaps it was the allure of Hollywood or the scented moonlit nights. Whatever the cause, the effect was intoxicating. The impossible seemed attainable.

Even Polly.

I pictured us dancing to a rhumba band at Ciro's, where the movie stars went; and when we arrived at our hotel, I prepared for the occasion with great vanity, splashing on some of Harry's cologne, even trimming my eyebrows. We had rooms at the Ambassador. Harry and I were in a wing above the swimming pool. Polly's room was across the hall. She flitted in and out, sewing a button on my last clean shirt, helping me with my tie. Harry phoned Ciro's.

"Did you get reservations?" Polly asked him.

He made a circle with his thumb and forefinger. "A ringside table."

"Ringside?" she said. "How on earth did you manage that?"

"Nothing to it," Harry said. "I told them I was Gene."

We burst into laughter. Everything we said or did

seemed hilarious. We barely noticed when Ellen came into the room and crossed to the dresser, where I was admiring myself in the mirror.

"It's your father, Skeets —" she said. "They just called from New York. He's had a stroke."

I reached for a chair. Suddenly everything seemed unreal, Ciro's, the hotel, the sounds of gaiety that drifted up from the pool. My father was ill, and I was three thousand miles from home.

"Gene is trying to arrange an airline priority," Ellen said. Because of the war, air travel had been sharply curtailed; civilians needed special approval. "He thinks Polly should go with you. You shouldn't be alone, and we can't get get along without Harry."

I spent the next few hours close to the phone. The circuits to the East were busy, and it was one o'clock before a call got through to Virginia.

"The damn war," I said angrily. "It's screwing up our whole lives."

Polly helped me pack. My "Pollyanna" score was in a folder on the dresser. I hoped she wouldn't see it.

"Honestly, Skeets," she said. "You've got more music than clothes."

It was remarkable how quickly everything was arranged. Gene decided that the band would make do with a four-man reed section while I was gone; A.C. Etter would play lead clarinet. Ellen would fill in for Polly.

"We'll stick to the simpler arrangements," she said. "I should be able to handle them."

When we were packed, Gus gave Polly an envelope

with money and our tickets. We would go by air to Philadelphia, then complete the trip by train and ferry-boat.

"It's the best I could do," he said. "Traveling's a bitch when there's a war on."

Basil went down to the lobby and held a cab for us. Half the band was waiting to say good-bye.

"I'll keep my fingers crossed, Skeets," Augie said.

"Me too," Buddy said.

Basil had tears in his eyes. "Good luck," he said, hugging me.

Gene put an arm around me. "Just get home to your family, Skeets," he said. "If not Saint Louis, we'll see you in Louisville."

"You've been swell, Gene," I said. "We'll try to make the date."

The cab pulled away from the hotel. It was very late, and the streets were nearly deserted. Polly was all business, checking our tickets, counting the money Gus had given us. There was no doubt who would be in charge of the trip.

"I'll wire your mother from the airport and tell her when to expect us. What did she say on the phone?"

"He's in a coma. The doctors don't have much hope."

"Was he at home when it happened?"

"No. He'd gone over to Virginia Beach on some errands. He came out of the bank and collapsed in the street."

"Well — say a prayer." She leaned over and straightened my tie. "You'll have to get some new shirts along the way. You'll want to look nice for your father."

A Silver Wand

It seemed strange to be leaving the tour. I'd never missed a performance before. We drove north, through the Hollywood Hills and down into the starlit San Fernando Valley. In the distance, the revolving airport beacon moved against the sky like a silver wand. I had a melancholy feeling that it was beckoning me to a journey that would change my life forever.

·11·
Old Point Comfort

The airliner was a twin-engined DC-3, silver with bright red markings. Polly and I were the only civilians aboard. The stewardess showed us how to work the safety belts. Neither of us had ever flown before, and we were both very nervous.

We took off just before dawn. The morning mist swirled off the propellers as the plane roared down the runway. As we cleared the San Gabriel Mountains, we could see the first orange tip of the sun rising in the east, while behind us Los Angeles and the coastal valleys were still shrouded in darkness. The first thing that struck me was how peaceful everything seemed from the air. Then we hit some turbulence, and I threw up — in one of the brown paper bags that had been provided for such problems.

"It's not like the train, is it?" Polly remarked.

It was a long, monotonous flight. We made stops at Denver, Omaha, Chicago, and Cleveland. I tried not to think of my father, but I kept wondering how he would look, what I would say to him, and my airsickness got worse. By noon, we were over the Great Plains. Five hours later, Polly spotted the Mississippi River.

I dozed intermittently, but the drone of the engines kept waking me. Dusk was creeping over Lake Erie as we left Cleveland and climbed toward the Appalachians.

"You need some sleep," Polly said to me. "Are there any Pullmans on the train to Cape Charles?"

"No. But you can pay extra and get a cabin on the ferry."

As we were letting down over Philadelphia, Polly took a wrinkled envelope from her purse.

"I found it when I was packing your things. Don't you think you'd better read it?"

It was the letter from my father, the one I'd received in Providence, still unopened.

"You read it," I said. "I'm not up to it."

Polly read the letter and gave a deep sigh. "Oh, Skeets, why didn't you read it when it first came? He's sorry about everything and wants to make up."

I forced myself to read it.

> *Dear Schuyler,*
>
> *Nearly all of the local boys have either enlisted or been drafted, and I expect the Army will soon be getting around to you, too, even with your eyesight problems.*
>
> *And so I wanted you to know that I realize now how stubborn I've been in opposing your career in music. The times have been so unsettled, I guess I've just been trying to hold the family around me. But it's your life, and you should do what you think is best. I'll be proud of you, whatever the results.*

I've been feeling a bit under the weather lately, but don't breathe a word to your mother. It's nothing a few days of fishing wouldn't cure. I hope you'll be coming home soon for a visit. We'll troll the marsh together, the way we used to do.

Meantime, take good care of yourself, and don't worry about the lumberyard. I'll manage just fine.

Love,
Dad

P.S. *We heard your broadcast from Hartford the other night. It's fine music, and it gave me a good feeling to know you're a part of it.*

There was a whining noise as the landing gear went down. The stewardess came back and asked us to fasten our safety belts. I slumped back in my seat, hating myself.

"I hope he doesn't die," I said aloud. "Damn it, I hope he doesn't die."

The trip to Cape Charles was a blur. There was a long wait for a taxi at the Philadelphia airport, and we had to run to catch the train. The train made stops all down the eastern shore of Chesapeake Bay — Dover, Pocomoke City, Chincoteague. Our coach was crowded and dirty and smelled of stale fruit. It was three o'clock when we pulled into Cape Charles, where the tracks ended and passengers for Norfolk had to cross the bay

by ferry. There was a pay phone on the pier. I hurried
to call home, while Polly boarded the ferry and arranged
accommodations. She was waiting for me at the purser's
office. The news must have been written in my eyes.

"Oh, Skeets, I'm so sorry." She took my hand and
held it tight. "When did it happen?"

"Around midnight," I said, feeling numb. "They
said it was very peaceful."

"I'll wire Gus when we get to Norfolk. Do you think
you could sleep?"

"I don't know. Did you get the cabins?"

"Just one. I don't want you to be alone."

"Let's stay on deck for a while," I said. "I'd like to
keep moving."

We strolled in silence around the upper deck. The
spray from the waves dampened our faces. When harbor
lights from the opposite shore came into view, we
started down to the cabin.

"Is that Norfolk?" Polly asked, pointing to the red
lights.

"Old Point Comfort," I said. "We make two stops
before Norfolk."

The cabin was down a passageway off the main deck.
It was a small, spare room — a chair, a washbasin, a
narrow berth with a porthole above it. I took off my
jacket and slumped onto the berth. Polly stood hesi-
tantly in the doorway, silhouetted in the dim light of
the passageway.

"Should I get us some sandwiches, Skeets? You
haven't eaten a thing since Los Angeles."

"Maybe later. I still feel sick from the plane."

She closed the door and left the lights off. The moon shone through the porthole. She took off her shoes and sat down next to me in the berth. The boat swayed and creaked. "If only I'd read that letter," I said. "He probably died thinking I hated him."

And finally the tears came. Polly rocked me in her arms.

"It's all right, Skeets." She stroked my hair. "Cry it out."

We crossed Chesapeake Bay that way, huddled in the berth in the darkness, rocking to the swaying movements of the boat. Then slowly, innocently, the rocking became something else — pressing, touching, embracing — shyly, tentatively, then urgently.

"Wait —" Polly whispered, and pulled away for a moment. There was a rustle of silk. "This is just for now, Skeets." Her voice trembled. "We'll never talk about it."

I helped her with her underthings. It was wrong, I knew, this lovely girl giving herself out of pity. I thought of the possible consequences, and a protest formed on my lips. But then her slender arms came up around me, and there was no helping either of us.

·12·
Truth and Justice

We stopped in Norfolk to buy me some new shirts, and then went straight to the funeral home. I thought sure I would go to pieces, but I didn't, mainly because of Polly and my mother. My mother insisted that the casket be kept closed. "He's not in that box," she said. "He's in our hearts." And so I never saw my father dead. It's easier when you don't see them dead.

After the funeral, the family gathered on the wide front porch — my two married sisters, assorted aunts and uncles, and my maternal grandparents. I had decided to come home after the tour and take over the lumberyard, at least for a while. My mother, however, wouldn't hear of it. I was to continue in my career; on that she was adamant. "We'll go on as before," she said, and announced that she intended to manage the lumberyard herself. She knew the business as well as anyone, she said, and it would keep her mind occupied.

And that was that.

We had four days in Princess Anne, the sleepy little courthouse town where I had been born and raised. The breathtaking Tidewater spring was in full bloom. The days were warm and fragrant, with a cool breeze at night. In the afternoons, my mother served lemonade under the sweetgum trees that shaded the house. It was a very old house, two-story brick, with high ceilings and a mansard roof. My room was above the pantry. Polly slept there during our visit, while I made a bed on the davenport in the parlor. It gave me a good feeling, knowing that Polly was in the house.

One of Polly's charms was her way of making the ordinary seem special. She fell eagerly into the household routine, doing the dusting, helping my mother tie up the wisteria vines, walking with me to the post office for the mail.

"She's a lovely girl," my mother said one morning when we had a few moments alone. "Is it serious?"

"No, Mama," I replied. "She's just a good friend."

She considered this, then shook her head. "I think not, Son," she said. "She never lets you out of her sight."

The band had wired flowers for the funeral. Two days later, a sympathy card arrived. Everyone in the band had signed it. Buddy had added a little message after his name.

> *My greetings from Uncle Sam arrived.*
> *Am trading my bass fiddle for a rifle.*

"Well," Polly said, "the quintet is down to a trio. At least you and Harry are safe."

"Can you picture Buddy with a rifle slung over his shoulder?" I said.

"No," she said. "It's dumb. Musicians don't make good soldiers."

The next day, a card arrived from Basil.

The new Down Beat *poll is out. We're number one. I repeat, number* ONE*!!!*

Polly read the message with tears in her eyes. "We dreamed of being number one," she said. "And now it doesn't mean anything. The darn war."

The war was never very far from Princess Anne. Planes from the great naval base at Norfolk were constantly overhead. The war continued to go badly. The Japanese had landed troops in the Aleutian Islands, near Alaska, and the Germans had taken a quarter of a million prisoners on the Russian front.

One day, Polly and I drove over to Virginia Beach. Sentries with rifles and guard dogs patrolled the beach. A line of warships was visible on the horizon, destroyers, I assumed, for German submarines were operating in the area. We bought salt-water taffy and strolled up the beach, past striped cabanas, all of them empty, and weathered old resort hotels. A formation of torpedo bombers came down the coast and veered out over the ocean. We sat on a stump of driftwood and watched the planes go out of sight. Just a few days ago, we had watched a similar scene on a Pacific beach. Princess Anne and the band seemed superfluous; the war was all that mattered.

"It's scary," Polly said, a little shiver running through her. "I can understand now why Gene volunteered."

"I know," I said. "You feel guilty for not being in it."

She scooped up a handful of sand. "Have you decided what you're going to do when we get back to New York?"

"Not really," I said. "The Philharmonic will be auditioning in August. I may try for it."

"What would you do in the meantime?"

"Maybe get a job with one of the pit orchestras. It depends on Harry. He's had a standing offer from a jazz joint on Fifty-second Street. If he takes it, we could share an apartment in Greenwich Village. What about you?"

"College or the job at Saint Mary's, I guess," she said. "I was counting on the combo. I haven't had time to decide which."

"What's Ellen planning to do?"

"Go back to Upper Darby, I guess. Unless something develops with Gene. She's invited me for a visit."

"It might be a good idea," I said. "It would give you a chance to figure things out."

"Maybe. But it seems a waste for everybody just to fade away. We should be making plans, and instead we're practically paralyzed. Look at Harry."

"Harry will be all right," I said. "He just hasn't gotten Sarah out of his system yet."

"It's not Sarah, Skeets. It's you."

"Me? But —"

"I know what you're going to say. That you admire Harry and depend on him. But it's really the other way around. Oh, he's witty and charming and has a way with the girls. But he relies on you to prop him up. Deep down, Harry is sort of a frightened little boy."

She stood up and brushed the sand from her skirt.

134

"I'm hungry." She took my hand and pulled me to my feet. "You can treat me to an ice cream cone."

Polly and I were together nearly every minute of those four days, but we made no mention of Old Point Comfort. Those whispered moments on the ferry had taken on a dreamlike quality. Had they really happened? One morning, however, when I went upstairs to get something from my room, I walked in as Polly was stepping out of her pajamas. There was no blushing, no hurried display of modesty. She simply smiled and continued with her dressing. I was glad she hadn't been embarrassed. A special bond now existed between us, although I couldn't have defined it.

On our last day, I took Polly on a tour of my boyhood places — the brick grammar school; Miss Pfeiller's studio, where I'd taken my first music lesson; an old fishing spot, where I used to string lines for catfish. It was in a marshy inlet on the edge of the Great Dismal Swamp. We rented a boat and rowed up the inlet. Cypress trees grew out of the water, and a tangle of crepe myrtle lined the banks. The rich smells made us drowsy.

"Is this where you used to go fishing with your father?" Polly said.

"Yes. We'd run lines and check them at dawn. That's the best time to come here, when everything's coming awake. It's like a symphony."

I rowed us deep into the marsh. Polly sat in the rear of the boat, her skirt bunched up and her legs stretched out in the sun. She watched a heron take flight from a cypress pool, then, without looking at me, said, "Skeets — I saw 'Pollyanna' when I was packing your things."

"I figured you did."

"Is it about me?"

I pretended to be busy with the oars. "Sort of," I mumbled.

"I can't think of a nicer compliment. Will you play it for me when it's finished?"

"That may be a while."

"That's all right," she said. "I can wait."

The sun was low over the marsh when we tied up. It was growing dark by the time we came across a field and through the scrub pine that bordered the backyard. A light in the kitchen window made a pleasant glow in the dusk.

"I just love this house," Polly said. "Will it be yours one day?"

"Probably. If I want it badly enough to buy out my sisters."

"And will you?"

"Of course," I answered. "It's my town and my state. I'll always come back here."

And for the first time in my life, I realized that that was truly how I felt.

The next day, we rode up to the railroad station in Norfolk. It rained all the way to St. Louis. We were delayed in Roanoke and again in Cincinnati while troop trains were cleared through. Ellen had wired us that the band would be taking a morning train to Louisville. I worried that we'd miss the connection.

It was a dull trip. We played a little gin rummy and read a few magazines, but mostly we just sat alone with our thoughts. Polly picked at her food in the diner and spent most of the trip gazing out the window. I'd seen her that way before, puzzling over some decision, even as small a thing as the selection of a new dress. She would be moody and withdrawn for days, then announce her decision and be her old self again.

We arrived in St. Louis two hours late. The band had already left for Louisville, but Gus had left Harry behind to wait for us.

"Skeeter!" he hollered through the crowd. "Pols!" — and it was as if we'd never been away.

"Hey, boy!" he said, slapping me affectionately on the back. "How're you holding up?"

"Pretty good, Harry." It felt good to see him again. "You know how it is. You roll with the punches."

"Sure, I know." He turned to Polly. "Pols, your nose is peeling."

Polly smiled demurely. "I got sunburned in a marsh."

"A marsh?" He nudged me with his elbow. "Skeeter, you ought to be ashamed of yourself. That's no place to take a lady.

"Come on," Harry went on, grabbing Polly's bags. "We've got to hustle over to the bus station. There isn't another train to Louisville till tonight."

We hurried to the taxi ramp, chattering a mile a minute.

"How did Ellen do?" Polly asked Harry.

"Terrific. She was a little nervous at first, but then she really got with it."

"Have she and Gene said anything about getting married?"

"Not a peep. But they slipped away to Palm Springs

137

our last night in L.A. and didn't get back till the wee hours."

"How's Gus?" I said.

"I think he's getting as sick of the road as we are. I was late for rehearsal yesterday, and he didn't bat an eye."

St. Louis looked bleak and grimy in the rain. Harry hailed a cab, and we all piled into it.

"Buddy wrote that he'd been drafted," Polly said.

"Did he tell you about me?" Harry said.

"What's there to tell?" I said.

He settled back in the seat and grinned. "Brace yourselves, kiddies," he said. "I've joined the navy."

"Draft dodger Harry Swanson joined the navy!" Polly exclaimed. "I don't believe it."

"See for yourself, Pols." He took a long envelope from his jacket pocket and handed it to her. "They've even got my fingerprints."

He had enlisted in Los Angeles, he told us, but he'd been thinking about it ever since that meeting with his father in Chicago. His file was being forwarded to New York, where he would be called up after the tour.

"Harry, Harry, Harry," Polly said, shaking her head. "I don't know whether to laugh or to cry."

"Did you try for something in music?" I asked.

"No, I didn't, Skeeter. I've applied for the flight cadets. I should be soloing by the end of the year."

The cab was pulling up at the bus station. I stared out the window and felt everything slipping away, the apartment in Greenwich Village, the ragtime concerto, the standing ovation in Carnegie Hall. Perhaps what

Polly had said about Harry was true. Even so, the prospect of our sticking together had been the only scrap of certainty left to me.

"Why did you do it, Harry?" I said. "Is this some kind of grandstand play to get Sarah back?"

"No, that's not it, Skeeter," he said. "Sarah's a dead issue. I'll admit that Sally Sengstock crossed my mind, but that's not it, either."

"Then *why*?" I pressed him.

"Hey, boy," he said, putting an arm around me. "Don't pick up your marbles. After all, you're the guy who made up my mind for me."

"Me?" I said. "How do you figure that?"

"Remember what you said back in New York?" he said. "About our being out of step? Well, you were right. Sure, I could've coasted along on my phony deferment, but what would I tell my kids when they ask me what I did in the war? Besides, I guess I'd like to find out what I'm made of."

The bus to Louisville was crowded, and we had to take separate seats. I took the only window seat left, next to a stout farm lady who was reading a newspaper that was filled with headlines about the war. As we crossed Illinois, the rain began to let up, and in Indiana, where the road wound in and out of the hills above the Ohio River, the day was bright and glistening.

I watched the river flowing toward the Mississippi, and felt as though I were approaching a milestone in my life. Basil had made a decision, Augie and Buddy had had decisions made for them, and now Harry had made a decision. And me — what did I want?

Music. In all its forms and expressions. I wanted to know it all, feel it all, experience it all — the jazz combos, the chamber ensembles, the great concert orchestras. Then having known it all, I wanted to add my contribution. I wanted to put the country to music, as Albéniz had put Spain to music, as I was trying to put Polly to music.

And so I would audition for the Philharmonic and wait for the draft board to scrape the barrel. Beyond that, I simply didn't know. It occurred to me that the tour had given me too strong a dose of life, and I was having trouble absorbing it. I was tired of buses, tired of war headlines, tired of everything. As I was thinking those dark thoughts, the bus stopped in a crossroads village, and the farm lady and several others got off. Polly moved to the empty seat beside me.

"Don't feel blue, Skeets," she said, giving my hand a little squeeze. "I haven't joined the navy."

Then Harry came back and sat on the armrest, full of funny stories about what had happened at the Palladium.

But I wasn't paying much attention. I was looking at Polly, and she was looking at me. And when a flush stole across her cheeks, my heart soared. The world suddenly seemed filled with truth and justice, even for short young men with thick glasses.

She had made her decision. Old Point Comfort hadn't been just pity, after all. I was sure of it.

·13·
The Sweetness of Time

We closed out the tour in Peoria, at the Père Marquette Hotel, and then did our final broadcasts from the Merchandise Mart studios in Chicago. The first show came off perfectly, but the rebroadcast for the Coast was a disaster. Polly missed a cue, and I squeaked a high note on our theme. Gene gave me an icy look, and Gus cornered me afterward in the booth.

"Gene sends his compliments, maestro," he said. "He's never heard a clarinet lead played with such originality."

"It was my reed, Gus," I said lamely. "My reed got dry between broadcasts."

"Oh, so your reed was dry, huh?" he said. "Well, do you suppose you could moisten it by the time we get back to New York?"

"You never let up, do you, Gus?" Harry snapped. "What a lousy outfit. No spirit."

"Spirit?" Gus poked a stubby finger in Harry's chest. "Discipline and spirit are the same thing, wise guy. Just wait'll you see how the navy dishes it out."

I had hoped that Harry's enlisting in the navy might

have improved his relationship with Gus, but it hadn't. Everyone seemed cranky. While Polly and I were away, induction notices had arrived for three of the others — A.C. Etter and two of the Mellow Birds.

"We're closing out the tour in the nick of time," Buddy said gloomily. "The whole band's gonna be afted-dray."

However, Basil, who had been doing research on army regulations, was his usual cheerful self.

"They only scalp you once," he said to Augie, trying to reassure him about basic training. "After that, you can let your hair grow out — but not too long."

"Will they let me use brilliantine?" Augie asked him.

"All you want," Basil said. "You can even use that new cream stuff. But you may have a problem with the army underwear. It's khaki."

"Khaki?" Augie said. "Why khaki?"

"Beats me," Basil said. "Maybe that way, if you have an accident, it won't show."

After the last broadcast, Augie and Buddy spent an hour composing a telegram to the Beasley twins.

"Make it real dramatic," Buddy urged Augie. "Make them want to give their all to the poor soldier boys."

"I know," Augie said. "We'll tell them we've volunteered for a dangerous secret mission."

"Hey, that's great," Buddy said. "We'll probably end up peeling spuds, but they'll never know that."

The following afternoon, we straggled aboard the Broadway Limited. Polly was coming down with a cold, Gus's bursitis was acting up, and Harry had sprained a finger. We had peaked, and we knew it. We were tired and played out and sick to death of pastrami sandwiches and chop suey joints.

"An orchestra is a scramble," Gus grumbled as he lugged his bags up the aisle of our Pullman. "Forever living out of a suitcase, and scared to death the bookings will run out. I should've stuck with the carnival."

"I'll bet it's not that way with the Philharmonic," I said.

"The Philharmonic scrambles, too," Gus said. "It's the secret of life. Scramble, scramble, scramble."

At dinner, Polly and I sat with Gene and Ellen. There was much well-wishing from the passengers as Gene made his way through the crowded dining car.

"Did you see the movie stars?" Ellen asked excitedly. "Orson Welles and Rita Hayworth are in the next car. They asked Gene for his autograph. I'll bet he's the most famous celebrity on the train."

Gene was in a serious mood. He talked of the war, and of music, and of the report in the *Chicago Tribune* that the Japanese had used the band's recordings during the fighting in the Philippines.

Polly frowned. "I don't understand," she said.

"They would play them on loudspeakers across the lines," Gene explained, "to make our troops homesick and weaken their will to fight."

I gazed out the window. The crack train rushed out of the city and through the vast industrial belt of northern Indiana. I imagined our music echoing out over the Bataan Peninsula, over the jungle rot and the corpses and the shot-down airplanes. *Now add a coupl'a flowers, a drop of dew.*

"Who knows?" Gene said. "When we start tangling with the Germans, maybe they'll use our recordings, too. Gives you a funny feeling, doesn't it?"

We ordered brook trout with tiny potatoes, boiled and buttered and sprinkled with parsley. Afterward, there was a party back in the observation lounge, Harry and I, Polly and Ellen, plus Gus and Basil, who drank a "Presbyterian" — ginger ale with a twist of lemon. Augie and Buddy joined us, briefly. Buddy noticed two unescorted girls sitting in the front of the car.

"There won't be anything like that in the army," he said as they excused themselves. "We gotta strike while we can."

The rest of us sat in the rear of the car, where there were couches and armchairs and table lamps that gave off a soft glow.

"Isn't Gene coming back?" Polly asked Ellen.

"He's up to his ears in work," Ellen said, "getting our accounts up to date."

There was the special shipboard quality that good trains always had, and we were able to put aside the knowledge that it was ending for us. Gus wondered out loud who would be number one in the *Down Beat* poll now that we were breaking up.

"Spike Jones," Basil joked.

We all laughed; Spike Jones and His City Slickers specialized in zany musical satires.

"Don't laugh," Gus said. "They're good. They can play us better than we can. Almost."

"Tommy Dorsey," Ellen suggested.

"Not a chance," Gus said. "He's got no feeling for the kids. Besides, he's an egomaniac and hard to work

144

for. You've got to be careful in this business. There are a lot of tyrannical bandleaders, and they'll exploit you."

"Is Gene a tyrant?" I asked him.

"Yes," Gus said. "For work. That's how we made number one. Work, work, work, Rehearse, rehearse, rehearse. And all those theories about music and civilization."

He signaled the porter for another round.

"Two for me," Harry said. "This is great Scotch."

"But in other respects," Gus went on, "Gene is the best of them all. I remember when he kept us going on pawn tickets and rented tuxedos. You wouldn't believe how many times his trombone was in hock —"

"And my diamond," Ellen put in.

"Yes, and Ellen's diamond," Gus said. "Oh, they were sweet times. The hungry times are always the happy times. But now — I don't know. The war is killing the bands. Artie Shaw and Eddy Duchin are being called up, and Clyde McCoy and his entire band are joining the navy. Pretty soon even I'll be in uniform."

We fell into silence. The train curved through the rolling hills of eastern Ohio. Lights were going out in the farmhouses. Even at night, there was a feeling of the strength and beauty of the land.

"It's a fantastic country, isn't it?" Polly said.

"Yes," Harry agreed. "It's a fantastic country and a fantastic train, and after tomorrow night, it'll be fantastic to sleep late and not worry where your laundry is."

The porter turned on the radio. *"This is KDKA,*

Pittsburgh." There was a jingle for Iron City Beer, and then they were playing one of our recordings, a ballad that featured Polly and the Mellow Birds.

> *So long, old friends,*
> *We may never meet again.*

Ellen started crying. "I feel so sad," she sobbed. "I knew it would end one day, but I feel so sad."

Harry wanted to keep the party going till Horseshoe Curve, but the fun had gone out of it. Basil had fallen asleep. Gene sent back word that he wanted to see Ellen, and then Polly and Gus became engrossed in a private conversation. Harry and I said our good nights and made our way forward through the sleeping train. Harry was in a silly mood, laughing and singing noisily. As we went by Gene's compartment, he started to knock on the door.

"Let's make sure he and Ellen aren't being naughty."

"Harry!" I grabbed his arm. "He'll kick us off the train!"

Our berths were already made up. We flipped for the lower. Harry lost, and as he kicked off his shoes and set them out for the porter to shine, he suddenly became serious.

"Well, old buddy," he said, throwing an arm around me. "I guess tomorrow it'll be bye-bye for us."

"I guess so, Harry."

"It's been swell, hasn't it? I mean, if we'd stayed at Juilliard, we'd be just a couple of conservatory freaks."

146

"Aw, come on, Harry. It's not as if we're never going to see each other again."

He grinned, but I could tell he was feeling very emotional.

"Yeah, we'll be in touch," he said. "I guess the damn war's been getting to me. Twenty years from now, we'll probably look back at all of this and laugh. Right?"

I felt my eyes filling with tears.

"Sure, Harry."

"Look, Skeeter. That night at Jiffy's — I'm sorry I knocked your glasses off."

"Forget it, Harry."

"But it's really been bothering me. I mean, we've been such good friends and all."

"Darn it, Harry," I said. "Will you please go to bed?"

"I guess I'd better." His own eyes were growing moist.

I boosted him into the upper.

"You know something, Skeeter?" He poked his head through the green Pullman curtains. "I'd give five years of my life to go back and do it all over again."

I crawled into my berth, the sheets cool and fresh, and propped up the pillows, so that I could look out the window. The train was pulling into Pittsburgh. The sky was orange from the glow of the blast furnaces. I thought of all the train windows I'd looked out since I joined the band. The Daylight up the San Joaquin Valley, and the Capitol Limited through the Blue Ridge at Harpers Ferry. The Hiawatha across Wisconsin, and the South Wind on my first trip to Florida, with me standing on the observation platform, breathing it all in, the sweet tropical air and the smell of the ocean. It had been my eighteenth birthday, and I had been overwhelmed by the vastness of my own land — the sagebrush and the jasmine, the jack pines and the palm fronds. It was a fine country, and maybe I'd better not wait for the draft board to scrape the barrel. The navy had a limited-duty program I might qualify for, open to men who couldn't meet the regular physical standards. And if the navy wouldn't take me, I could always sign up with a USO troupe.

"Skeets," a voice whispered. "Are you still awake?"

I stirred from my reverie. It was Polly, in pajamas and robe, peering through the curtains.

"Polly. Is something wrong?"

"No. I just couldn't sleep, that's all. Are you all right, Skeets?"

"Yes, I'm okay. A little sad, though."

"I know. The party turned into a wake. Is Harry asleep?"

"Finally."

"Then it's all right if we talk?"

"Sure."

I held back the curtains and made room for her at the foot of the berth.

"Harry was so funny tonight," she said. "Do you realize it's the first time he's gotten tight since Jiffy's?"

"I think he's starting to get his old confidence back," I said. "It's funny about Harry, isn't it? He was always so sure of himself, and the tour turned out so lousy for him."

"Maybe not," Polly said. "There may be a surprise

for him in New York. I made a phone call while we were in Chicago."

"To Sarah?"

"I'd better not say. It isn't a hundred percent sure, but it's special."

She curled up next to the window and wrapped her arms around her legs. The train was settling into its long pull through the mountains. Darkened towns made fleeting silhouettes in the moonlight, then were swallowed up in the soft Allegheny night.

"I've got another surprise," Polly said. "Guess what? I'm going to be adopted."

"*Adopted!*" I sat up straight. "By whom?"

"Gus and Sadie."

"Well, I'll be —"

"I know it seems dumb, being adopted when you're nearly nineteen years old, but it's what I want. Actually, there were two offers — Gus and Sadie, and Gene and Ellen."

"Gene and Ellen? Then the wedding bells are for real this time?"

"Yes. Isn't it wonderful? They're going to be married before Gene reports for duty."

"When did all this happen?"

"In California. They were going to keep it a secret till we got back to New York."

"We'll have to throw a party."

"There's no time. We'll be in New York in six or seven hours."

"I'll talk to Harry. He'll think of something. When will Gus be passing out our checks?"

"At breakfast."

"Maybe we could do something then."

"We'll be rolling in money," she said. "We're getting a huge bonus, and Gus is even refunding all of Harry's fines."

"That Gus." I shook my head and smiled. "Wouldn't it be nice if he and Harry buried the hatchet before we break up?"

"Yes, that would be lovely. Deep down, Gus is just a gruff old papa bear. I can't wait to get to Toledo. I'll have a home of my own. A real home."

"But are you sure you're making the right choice, Polly? I mean, you and Ellen have been like sisters."

"It wouldn't be any good, Skeets. Gene has driven himself so hard, he doesn't know who he is."

"Ellen will straighten him out."

"I know," she agreed. "But I'd just be in the way. It's different with Gus and Sadie. They really need me. Gus is going to buy a movie theater and give up traveling. There's a little college near their house. I'm going to go to school and lead a normal life for a change."

"No Sister Angela?" I said.

She smiled. "I think I'll be able to manage without her. Will you come visit me?"

"Sure. I'll bring you flowers and candy and promise Gus not to keep you out late."

"Will you really?" She giggled. "That might be risky."

"How so?"

"Flowers and candy could — lead to things."

"Such as?"

"Oh-h, impetuous things . . ."

After a pause, she went on matter-of-factly. "You're my roots now, Skeets. I'd be lost without you."

"You're not just saying that because of — you know, Old Point Comfort?"

"No. Because of everything. Boston and Saint Mary's and being with you in Princess Anne. It's as if we've been drifting toward each other since the tour began."

"I know," I said. "I've had the same feeling, only it was too much to hope for. I mean, of all the guys you could have —"

"Oh, Skeets, aren't you ever going to stop belittling yourself?"

"Aw, come on, Polly."

"But you have so many good qualities. You're kind and true and gentle. You know exactly where you're going and how to get there. One day you'll be an important composer, and maybe I'll have had something to do with it."

She leaned forward and kissed me lightly on the lips.

"But there's one thing," she said. "You won't rush me, will you? I know it sounds dumb after what happened on the ferry, but I want life to slow down for a while."

"It isn't dumb, Polly," I said. "Besides, there probably won't be any time to rush you. I'm going to try to enlist in the navy's limited-duty program when we get back to New York. That, or sign up with the USO."

"Oh-h." Her voice was almost inaudible. "So you've made a decision, too."

"I guess we've all made decisions."

She seemed hurt. "It's not because of Harry, is it? You're not doing it just to keep up with him?"

"It's got nothing to do with Harry," I said. "It's — well, I really can't explain it."

She turned to the window. The red blur of a crossing signal flashed by.

"Well—" she said. "I've waited this long for a family. I guess I can wait till the war's over for the next milestone in my life."

When she said that, my heart thumped. I had been in love with Polly since the day I met her. What was happening seemed too good to be true, and I knew I was handling the situation badly.

"But even if I get called up," I said, "it wouldn't be right away. Maybe I could go out to Toledo and help you get settled."

She smiled with relief. "I was hoping you would," she said. "If the navy takes you, where would you be stationed?"

"Great Lakes, probably. That's near Chicago."

"I'll send you cookies."

"Homemade?"

"Naturally. All Saint Mary's girls are good cooks."

"You're full of surprises," I said.

"So are you." She stretched her arms and yawned. "It'll be so nice, getting to know each other away from the band."

"You're tired," I said. "We'd better pack it."

"Skeets —" she said softly. "Could I sleep with you tonight? I mean — just sleep?"

"Holy cow, Polly," I said. "You sure strain a guy's gallantry."

I fluffed the pillows and held back the covers. She slipped off her robe and snuggled in beside me. Her cheeks were scrubbed and shiny, and there was a faint scent of soap in her hair.

"Skeets, how many times have we stayed up late talking like this?"

"I don't know. A hundred, probably."

"It's a good start, isn't it?"

"Yes, Polly. It's a fine start."

I pulled the covers up around us. The train was rounding Horseshoe Curve. The tracks behind us gleamed like strands of silver in the moonlight. We would wind down out of the mountains to Philadelphia, and then begin the fast, straight run to New York — the final run. I felt Polly's legs against mine, warm and smooth. There would be trouble along the way, I knew, for we were opposites in so many ways. But that was all right. We would make it. In the sweetness of time, in the fullness of our possibilities — we would make it.

"Skeets," Polly whispered.

"Yes, Polly?"

"Are you sure Harry's asleep?"

"He's out like a light."

She reached under the covers for my hand.

"I guess it's silly to wait. You might be away for a long time . . ."

And then there was only the muted clicking of the rails as the train sped into the night.

Clickety-clack, we're coming back.
Clickety-clack, we're coming back.

·14·
A National Institution

Reporters and photographers lined the platform as the sleek, Tuscan-red Broadway Limited glided to a stop at Penn Station. There was the popping of flashbulbs and much confusion and scrambling for luggage. The news of Gene and Ellen's marriage plans and of Polly's adoption spread quickly through the crowd. The photographers took shots of Gene with Ellen, of Gene with Polly and Gus, of the four of them strolling up the platform, waving.

"Where will the wedding be held, Ellen?" asked the man from the *Times*.

"Upper Darby."

"And the honeymoon?"

Ellen blushed. "Fort Meade," she answered. "I'll be a camp follower till Gene is shipped overseas."

And then the attention focused on Polly.

"Polly, about your career —"

"I'm going to go to college and sing in the *a cappella* choir."

Ellen broke away for a moment and came over to Harry and me.

"That was a lovely party the two of you arranged at breakfast," she said. "How did you manage to get flowers at that hour?"

"The conductor wired ahead," Harry said. "They were waiting at North Philadelphia."

"I should have known." She gave us each a hug. "The famous wise guys. It's been so good knowing you, watching you grow —"

A tear ran down her cheek.

"Aw, come on, Ellen," I said gently. "This is no time for tears."

"I know." She dabbed at her eyes. "It's just that I'm so proud of us all."

And then the photographers were clamoring for more pictures.

"Kiss her, Gene!" a newsreel cameraman hollered.

Harry and I watched the proceedings with wide smiles.

"Was it a good tour?" the reporter from *Variety* asked us.

"Yes," Harry replied. "It was a very good tour. Wasn't it, Skeeter?"

I looked across the platform. Gene seemed more relaxed than I had ever seen him, and there was a new look of purpose and confidence in Polly's eyes. I was filled with a warm feeling of love and pride.

"Yes," I said. "It was the best tour of all."

"I understand some of the sidemen have received their draft notices," he said.

"Six," I said. "And another has enlisted in the navy."

As I answered his questions, he kept glancing over my shoulder, with an increasingly puzzled expression.

"I'm sorry," he apologized, shaking his head. "I seem to be seeing double."

I turned around and beheld for the first time the Beasley twins, identical in every respect, clothes, hairdos, shoes. They were talking animatedly with Augie and Buddy, who were smiling happily. In a word, the Beasley twins were stacked, and it occurred to me that Augie and Buddy would have something to dream about no matter what remote outpost the army sent them to.

"Harry and Skeets," Augie said, turning to face us, "I want you to meet Dora and Donna."

"Which is which?" I asked, smiling.

"I'm Donna," said one twin, extending her hand. "Pleased to meetcha."

"Likewise, I'm sure," said the other, who obviously was Dora.

"How do we tell you apart?" Harry said.

Buddy grinned. "There are ways," he said.

"Oh, Buddy," Dora said, blushing and slapping his face playfully.

"Will you be at the farewell performance tonight?" I asked the girls.

They seemed to talk in tandem, in a heavy Brooklyn accent.

"We can't," said Donna.

"We've got jobs," said Dora.

"At a war plant in Flatbush," explained Donna.

"The swing shift," added Dora.

"I'm a riveter," said Donna.

"I'm an inspector," said Dora.

"She inspects what I rivet," said Donna.

It was like watching a tennis ball go back and forth over the net. Augie and Buddy were handing their luggage to a redcap, instructing him to take it to the Vanderbilt.

"Mrs. Beasley has invited us for lunch," Augie said. "Check us into the hotel, will you, Skeets? We'll see you later."

"Don't be late tonight," I said to them.

"So we're late?" Buddy said. "What's Gus gonna do, fire us?"

We all laughed.

The photographers were still snapping pictures as we crossed the great high-vaulted concourse to the tunnel that ran under Seventh Avenue to the hotel. Bellhops hurried out for our luggage. There was a huge *Good Luck, Gene* floral arrangement in the center of the lobby, and another outside the Emerald Room. The hotel staff burst into applause as Gene and Ellen came into the lobby, Ellen smiling and radiant, Gene with an arm draped loosely over her shoulders. The manager rushed forward with a bouquet of roses for Ellen and a stack of congratulatory telegrams for Gene.

"We had to move the performance to the ballroom," he said, patting his brow nervously. "The demand for tickets was just too great."

At the desk, Harry and I checked in Augie and Buddy, and then we took an elevator up to the fourteenth floor. Our room was filled with a fragrance of freshly cut flowers. As we unpacked, the bell captain came by with a basket of fruit. He asked for our autographs.

"For my son," he said. "He says the band will go down in history."

Harry flopped onto one of the beds and scratched his head.

"I've never seen anything like it," he said. "I never realized we were this big."

We finished unpacking and sent our suits down to be sponged and pressed. It was a clear, sunny day. I could see Central Park, the George Washington Bridge, and beyond, the Palisades.

"I just remembered," Harry said from his bed. "Gene didn't say anything about rehearsal."

I closed the Venetian blinds and stretched out on the other bed. "Why should he?" I said. "There's nothing left to rehearse."

We slept till late afternoon. At four, Augie and Buddy came by our room to report on their day with the Beasley twins.

"We had a great time," Augie said. "Mrs. Beasley thinks we're regular gentlemen."

"We saw the factory where they work," Buddy said. "Big place that makes parts for those B-seventeen bombers. We're going to meet the girls when they get off tonight."

"Hot time tonight, huh?" Harry said.

Buddy seemed affronted by Harry's remark.

"Dora is really a very nice girl, Harry," he said. "I don't push it with her." It was evident that the Beasley twins had evolved from the casual to the serious.

There was a steady parade in and out of our room that afternoon. Polly and Basil came by, taking up a

collection for a wedding gift for Gene and Ellen and
alerting us to an impending visit by Gene and Gus.

"What the hell did we do now?" Harry said.

"It's nothing like that," Basil said. "They want to
say good-bye to all the guys in private."

When they came, Gene had a little gift for each of
us, a set of three records — the six sides we'd recorded
the first day of the tour, along with a personal note of
thanks.

"Well —" he said, smiling. "We made it to the top,
thanks to each of you. An orchestra is only as good as
its musicians. I was blessed with the best."

He gave Harry and me each a warm handshake.

"It was an important day for me, that Sunday afternoon I decided to drop by Juilliard," he said. "Skeets,
Harry — you've been superb."

Then, turning to Augie and Buddy, he said, "Augie,
Buddy, I want each of you to give me one dollar. No
questions asked."

"What's the deal, Gene?" Augie said.

Each of them gave him a dollar bill; in return, he
gave them each a slip of paper. "Buddy, you now own
a bass fiddle," he said. "Augie, the trap drums are yours.
These are your bills of sale. I'll have the instruments
shipped to Elkhart."

"Well, I'll be damned —" Augie said.

Buddy had tears in his eyes.

"I think this is the nicest thing that's ever happened
to me," he said. "Thanks, Gene."

"Quit your sniveling, Buddy," Gene said, and put an
arm around Basil.

"Basil," he said, "on every date we played, the promoter remarked how efficiently we got set up. Did you know that Benny Goodman once tried to hire you away from me?"

"Benny *Good*man?" Basil said, his eyes wide. "I never knew that."

"Of course you didn't," Gene said, smiling. "I never told you. Benny was willing to pay you thirty-five a week."

"You can go to the top in this business, Basil," Gene went on. "And to help you get there, you've now got a scholarship to any conservatory or school of music of your choice. I'm mailing all the information you need to your mother."

For the first time since we'd met him, Basil was speechless. Then he let out a great yell and began jumping up and down.

"Whoopee!"

He hugged Gene, he hugged Gus, he hugged everyone.

"A conservatory!" he said excitedly. "Wow! Maybe I'll go to Juilliard like Skeets and Harry."

When he finally settled down, it was Polly's turn.

"Polly," Gene said, "your farewell present has four feet. Gus, tell the bellboy to come in."

A bellhop had been waiting in the hall, holding a small cage that contained a puppy — a male, solid black with a white patch on its snout.

"A dog!" Polly cried, her eyes glistening. She threw her arms around Gene. "Oh, thank you, thank you! It's the most wonderful gift I've ever received!"

She opened the cage and let the puppy lick her face. "What kind is he?" she asked.

"Who knows?" Gus said. "We rescued him from a dog pound up in the Bronx."

"What're you going to name him, Polly?" Buddy asked.

"How about 'Shadow'?" Basil suggested. "He's all black."

Polly thought for a moment. Then her eyes lit up. " 'Combo,' " she said.

"Hey, that's a swell name," Augie said.

"Speaking of the combo," Gus said. "I want you guys —"

Gene interrupted him. "I'll let you have a few minutes alone with them, Gus," he said. "The colonel will be here any minute."

"Okay, Gene," Gus said. "I'll catch up to you."

He began again. "As I was saying," he said, "I want all of you guys to get through the war in one piece, understand, because when it's over, I'm gonna finance your combo."

"Are you serious, Gus?" I said.

"Of course I'm serious," he said. "I never joke about money. I'll take fifteen percent off the top, same deal I've got with Gene."

"It's a deal," Augie said, beaming.

"What do you figure the tab at, Skeets?" Gus asked me.

"Seventy-eight hundred," I said. "That's without vibes."

"How much with vibes?"

"Eighty-five hundred."

"Make it with vibes," he said. "I only invest in first-class combos. What about a car?"

"A used Packard or La Salle."

"Make it a new Packard. Breakdowns on the road can be murder. What do you figure for contingencies?"

"About thirteen hundred."

"Not enough. Better cost it out at fifteen thousand, total. You'll run into a lot of problems, and it's nice to have plenty of dough to fall back on."

"Gus," I began, "I don't know what to say —"

"This means a hell of a lot to us, Gus," Buddy broke in.

"Yeah," Augie said. "We'd given up, but now we've got something to shoot for, even with the war."

"Not another word," Gus said. "A deal's a deal. Now Gene's waiting on me, and I've got to take the canine Combo down to the bell captain. We're shipping him to Toledo tomorrow."

As Gus was preparing to leave, Harry stepped forward and held out his hand. The moment Polly and I had hoped for had finally come. "I'll be going up to Poughkeepsie in the morning, Gus," he said awkwardly. "But I want you to know it's been grand. I mean, I've griped a lot, but it's been grand."

"You don't have to tell me, wise guy." Gus pulled Harry to him in a burly hug. "You've got class, real class. I'm expecting big things of you, so take good care of yourself in the navy. Okay?"

Harry smiled. "Okay, Gus," he said.

Basil picked up Combo's cage.

"I'll run it down to the bell captain for you, Gus," he said.

"Thanks, kid," Gus said.

He waddled to the door, trying to conceal his eyes, which were wet with tears.

"Nine o'clock sharp," he said on the way out. "And get those fruity shoes shined."

When Gus and Basil had gone, the rest of us all sat down and tried to absorb what had happened.

"I can't believe it," I said. "In just a few minutes, all of our problems got solved."

"Except the war," Buddy said.

"Yes," I said. "Except the war."

"Old Stone Face has really ruined his image," Harry said.

"Old Cream Puff, you mean," Polly said.

Augie got to his feet. "Hey, Buddy," he said. "Let's go back to our room and call that factory. Maybe they'll let us talk to Dora and Donna."

"Swell idea," Buddy said. "Oh, boy. Wait'll we tell 'em the news."

"See you guys later," Augie called back. "Don't forget to shine those fruity shoes, Harry."

When the door closed behind them, the room suddenly seemed empty. I looked out the window, at dusk creeping over the towers of Manhattan, and felt a letdown. Harry and Polly seemed to feel it, too.

"Well, kiddies —" Harry said after a while. "Shall we partake of an evening repast? Maybe Pasquale's?"

"I'm really not very hungry," Polly said. "How about a snack over at our coffee spot?"

We had soup and sandwiches at the place opposite Penn Station. We didn't feel like eating and didn't feel like talking. Walking back to the Vanderbilt, we noticed the hotel marquee.

Tonight
THE GENE MARKHAM ORCHESTRA
Farewell Performance

"It's funny," Harry said, "but I never thought we were that special. For two years, we've been on a treadmill, bouncing around the country in trains and buses, trying to measure up to Gene's standards and never quite making it. And now it turns out that we're some kind of national institution. How did it happen, Skeeter?"

I didn't have an answer, but Polly summed it up quite simply.

"We gave it our best, Harry," she said.

We stood in silence, staring up at the marquee.

"I feel lousy," Harry said.

"So do I," I said. We turned into the hotel. "Come on, let's see who's in the bar."

·15·
One More Time!

There is a legend about that last performance. About how we all showed up cranky and depressed and half tight. About the bickering, and how Gene lost his temper with the army colonel who wanted to delay the formal presentation of Gene's captain's commission until the last set, when we would be on a coast-to-coast radio hook-up. About the giggling and cutting up in the brass section, and how Augie cracked a stick making a clumsy rim shot.

"Furioso," I could hear him muttering between numbers. "Molto furioso."

We played petulantly, ineptly. It was as though we had left it all out on the road, somewhere between the Panther Room and Horseshoe Curve, and even the crowd sensed that our hearts weren't in it.

"I wish to hell it was over," Harry said as we broke for intermission.

"And we're supposed to be number one," I said.

"Poor Gene," Polly said. "And he wanted us to go out in style."

"Don't worry," Basil said. "You'll get on the pace. Even Beethoven must've had his off moments."

"Let's take a walk," I suggested. "Maybe some fresh air will perk us up."

As we left the ballroom, Polly spotted a familiar face in the crowded mezzanine. She slipped her hand into mine.

"Hang on to your hat," she whispered. "Here comes the surprise."

It was Sally Sengstock.

"Hey, that's the girl from the prom," Basil said.

Sally stood on her toes and waved. "Harry!" she called. "Over here!"

Harry's mouth fell open. "Well, I'll be —" He elbowed a path through the crowd. "Skeeter," he said with a wide grin. "I have a hunch my love life is about to take a turn for the better."

Sally was wearing a simple seersucker dress that made her stand out in the crowd. There was something reassuring about her, I thought, something solid and wholesome. I had a feeling that we were going to get to know her quite well.

"I tried to see you earlier," she said to Harry, smiling, "but I couldn't get a ticket."

"But what are you doing in New York?" Harry asked her.

"My father's attending the hardware convention," she said. "Remember?"

"Gee, that's swell," Harry said, shuffling around like a schoolboy. "Really swell."

Polly and I watched in amusement as a romance unfolded at a breathtaking pace.

"Hey, why don't you come up to Poughkeepsie with

me tomorrow and meet my family?" he said. "You could stay overnight."

"I'd have to ask my father, but I'm sure it would be all right."

"I've joined the navy, you know."

"Yes, I heard."

"But how —"

"A little bird told me." Sally glanced at Polly and winked. "When do you have to report?"

"In two weeks."

"Two weeks is a long time, actually. Maybe you could make a trip to Galesburg. My mother's dying to meet you."

Gus came out to round us up. We sneaked Sally into the ballroom, and Basil found her a chair close to the bandstand.

"Skeeter," Harry said, "you'd better start packing We'll be making a fast trip to Illinois."

I had put off telling Harry about Polly and me; I wasn't sure how he'd react. But now I drew a deep breath and took the plunge.

"Sorry, Harry," I said. "You're on your own. I'll be busy in Toledo."

"Toledo?" He stood back and gave me a puzzled look. "You mean — you and Polly?"

I grinned self-consciously.

"You and *Polly*?" he repeated. Then his eyes lit up. "Why, of course! It's been Skeets and Polly all along, only we've been too dumb to notice."

"That's not all," I said. "I'm going to enlist."

"But you're four-F."

"The navy has a limited-duty program. They might take me."

He gave my glasses a playful tug. "With those eyes," he said, "how could they resist?"

We went around to the stairway that led up to the bandstand. A crew from the radio network had arrived. Basil helped the engineer place the microphones. Harry turned and waved to Sally. She blew him a kiss, and suddenly I felt very hopeful about the future, both for Harry and for me. There would be warmth and laughter and happy good-byes at Grand Central. And I thought what a fine experience the tour had been. We had grown a little. Not much, perhaps, but enough to look ahead with a clear understanding of our responsibilities.

"Okay, wise guys." It was Gus again. "If you'll kindly hustle your bustles."

And then we assembled for the last time, the All-American boys and the Girl Next Door, the musicians in two-tone blue and Polly like a breath of spring in white chiffon. To our surprise, Gus sat down on a riser in the rhythm section and motioned for Ellen and Basil to join him. "Gene wants us all onstage for the last set," he said.

Basil wrapped his arms around his knees, exposing the full length of his bright argyle socks.

"Basil!" Ellen whispered. "You're wearing those damn socks!" — and he scrunched his legs under him, so that the socks wouldn't show.

We horsed around, waiting for our cue. It was midnight in New York, eleven in Chicago, and nine o'clock on the Coast. The engineer raised an arm.

"From the Hotel Vanderbilt in New York City —"

There was some giggling in the brass section and the clatter of a mute being dropped. Then Gene turned to face us.

"For us," he said. "Let's show them who we are. Uh-one and uh-two —"

And it began — softly, sweetly, the music flooding out over the ballroom like moonbeams, one number after another, as if our instruments had taken charge and were playing themselves. At first, I thought it was just my imagination. Then I glanced around and saw a faraway look in everyone's eyes, and I knew we were reaching for it, as though it had finally sunk in that the road ended here, and we were reaching for it one more time, proudly, in a dazzling display of musicianship — stardust and saxophones and Polly bathed in a blue spotlight.

We were in superb control. Through the ballads first, then into the instrumentals, gradually picking up the beat, but holding ourselves in check with an ingrained sense of discipline. Then in the middle of "One O'Clock Jump," Harry went into an improvisation that gave me goosebumps. I looked up at Gene, expecting the inevitable reprimand — *"Observe the markings!"* But he just grinned, picked up his trombone, and went into an improvisation of his own. We let out a yell. The brakes were off! The beat quickened, the crowd roared, and as we set out to make the critics eat their reviews — it finally happened.

We played flawlessly, inventively, swinging as no other band had ever swung before. Five minutes, ten, with the engineer frantically signaling for the sign-off and the announcer waving him down.

Gene showcased every ensemble, every soloist, letting us soar as high as our spirits would carry us. When I thought we were ready to finish, he waved a cue to Augie and Buddy.

"Fiddlesticks!" he called to them.

Buddy, with a happy grin, quickly twirled his bass around, so that Augie could play the strings from his place at the drums, sometimes playing the high-hat cymbal with one stick, the A string with the other. The crowd broke into a tremendous round of applause, and several couples started jitterbugging.

The full band came in for a final riff, and then Gene threw it to Harry to wrap up, which he did with a *cadenza* that was a recapitulation of the band's history — quick little quotes of our most famous numbers, in decreasing tempo, first the instrumentals, then the ballads. Gene sensed where Harry was leading us and brought the band in softly under the piano. And then we drifted effortlessly into our theme, that lovely, lilting theme that had been such an important part of our lives.

Coupl' a jiggers of moonlight and add a star,
Pour in the blue of a June night and one guitar.

And so in the end, the last was the best. The theme expressed it all, everything we had learned, the artistry and the discipline and the special touch that was ours and ours alone.

We played it over and over, enlarging it for our memories. Then Gene signaled a cut and asked the entire band to stand. The applause was thunderous. Polly came to my side and took my hand as we bowed to the crowd.

It was over.